"Can I hold him? love to meet little…

She left the question open, hoping the firefighter would come up with a name. The man cringed. "Okay, I'll think of something while you hold him as he screams," he said.

Tessa chuckled. "I'll see if I can soothe him."

She held the baby and sang the song her own foster mother had crooned to her when she was young.

The small boy stopped crying immediately. Luke's mouth dropped open. "No one has been able to do that."

Tessa grinned. "Well, I guess he likes the both of us."

She took a moment to study him. The tall firefighter looked polished despite the late hour. His uniform bore no wrinkles and was tucked perfectly into place.

The social worker came back into the room. "I have all the paperwork done. You can take him home now if you'd like, Tessa," Sierra said.

Luke's shoulders slumped at that. It seemed the firefighter was having a hard time letting go.

Julie Brookman is a former preacher's kid who started her career after college as the manager of a bookstore, later becoming a journalist and public relations specialist. She has spent her whole life with her nose in a book and loves stories with happily-ever-afters. Besides writing sweet and inspirational romance novels, Julie enjoys hiking, reading and belting out show tunes at the top of her lungs (which leads to strange looks from other drivers she passes). Julie lives in Michigan with her three awesome kids and her kitty, Pepper Potts. Email her at julie@authorjuliebrookman.com.

Books by Julie Brookman

Love Inspired

His Temporary Family
His Unexpected Baby Blessing

Visit the Author Profile page at LoveInspired.com for more titles.

HIS UNEXPECTED BABY BLESSING

JULIE BROOKMAN

LOVE INSPIRED
INSPIRATIONAL ROMANCE

LOVE INSPIRED®
INSPIRATIONAL ROMANCE

ISBN-13: 978-1-335-93711-7

His Unexpected Baby Blessing

Recycling programs
for this product may
not exist in your area.

Love Inspired
22 Adelaide St. West, 41st Floor
Toronto, Ontario M5H 4E3, Canada
www.LoveInspired.com

Printed in Lithuania

MIX
Paper | Supporting
responsible forestry
FSC® C021394

Verily I say unto you, Inasmuch as ye have done it
unto one of the least of these my brethren,
ye have done it unto me.
—*Matthew* 25:40

I dedicate this book to all the first responders
who are often the heroes of little ones
at some of the worst moments of their lives.
They are lucky to have you. We all are.

Chapter One

It was a rare occurrence that the fire station was quiet. Even during the middle of most nights, they would get calls to serve in their small suburban Crossroads Junction, Colorado, community and have to be on the truck at a moment's notice.

But every once in a while, there was peace. The crew would take the opportunity between calls in the wee hours of the morning to crash in the beds at the station, with one person volunteering to stay on watch in case anything happened. The guys would sometimes blurt out "Not it" loudly, and the loser would have to skip their nap. Or they would draw names from a hat. Sometimes, it was whoever was on the captain's bad side that week.

Tonight, however, Luke Russell had volunteered for the spot. He did it at least once every few weeks. He enjoyed the peace and quiet, the only sounds being the ventilation system circulating air through the building and the squeak of his shoes on the shiny floor. This week had been busy, with lots of calls that had pulled them all over town. Not only putting out fires but also rescuing cats from trees and helping stranded hikers who had been overly ambitious in their climbs.

Luke loved his crewmates, but their chaotic energy was draining sometimes. So tonight, he was enjoying the silence of the station while he gave the fire engine a polish. Neat, orderly and calm. That was the way he liked things. Being a firefighter rarely allowed for peaceful work shifts, but he compensated with solitude in abundance at home.

The utter silence of the station was jarringly interrupted by a sudden alarm in the night. It wasn't the fire alarm—*that* was loud enough to wake everyone from their beds. It was more like a buzzing noise and a beeping, coming from the front of the station. Luke's entire body froze at the sound.

Because of their training session last week with a local social worker, Luke knew exactly what that noise was. He rushed to the drop box near the entrance of the station, knowing every moment was precious. Opening the box automatically turned off the alarm; inside, there was a tiny bundle wrapped in blankets. And it was crying.

"Hey there, little one. You have a loud holler for someone so small," Luke said as he scooped the baby up and held it in his arms.

The crying immediately stopped, and he gazed down softly at the new arrival. His heart broke at the thought of this little one all alone in the world. "Let's just check you out and wait a few more minutes to make sure your mama doesn't change her mind and come back for you."

The safe-haven baby drop was a miracle of an invention, in Luke's opinion. Long gone were the days where people would leave infants they couldn't care for in a basket on a doorstep, exposed to the elements. In an effort to curb young parents leaving their newborns somewhere dangerous, the government passed safe-haven baby laws, where they could drop their infants off at hospitals or fire stations with no questions asked and no charges for abandonment.

To help make it anonymous and safe, these locations added the boxes to keep the abandoned babies warm while an alarm sounded on the inside for someone to come help as soon as possible.

Luke visually inspected the baby quickly before taking its vitals. It looked to be about a few months old, from what he could tell. Once he'd ensured the little wiggle worm of a baby was stable, he wrapped it in a blanket and cradled it against his chest. It was a chilly night, and the station always had a breeze going through it. Little gurgles of happiness emitted from the baby when Luke bounced it gently. A grin formed on his face when he realized that the baby was most content in his arms. *Maybe I'm a baby expert*, he thought, pride filling him. *I must be a natural, because I don't spend time with little ones often.*

His friends had babies, but Luke never went out of his way to hold them. Yet this tiny human made a point of crying every time he set it down. And while there was something warm and settling about holding the baby to his chest, he couldn't do this all night. He had to follow procedure. He set the baby down next to him on the couch and reached for his phone so he could call his captain upstairs and wake everyone. But that wasn't needed because the baby notified the crew for him.

Wails filled the station the moment the little tyke left Luke's chest. It wasn't long until his fellow crew members appeared, sleepy eyed.

"Whoa, a baby? I know we did that safe-haven stuff, but I don't think I've ever been here when we've gotten one," his friend Sam said.

Luke held the tiny package out to him. "You want to hold it?"

The baby let out a wail when he held it out toward his friend. Everyone in the room cringed at the sound. Luke snuggled the baby close again, and it fell silent.

Sam shook his head. "Looks like you've got it handled. I get enough screams daily from my newborn at home."

Their captain chuckled and patted Sam on the back. "That makes you the expert in the building, though."

The rookie, Eric, stepped forward with his arms held out. "I'll hold it while they get the ambulance fired up." The emergency medical team members hurried over to notify the hospital they were coming and start their ambulance.

"Right, I was getting to that," Luke said. The first step in this process, besides making sure the baby was stable, was getting it to the hospital's medical staff for further examination. The Department of Children's Safety would be contacted from there to find a home for the baby. Luke felt a little tug in his heart at the thought of not knowing what would happen to this little one in the future.

As soon as Eric took the baby, it cried. "I think I broke it," the young man said with panicked eyes. "Someone else take it."

Another firefighter stepped up to take the tiny bundle. But the crying didn't stop. The crew members all passed the baby to each other, but none of them could soothe the wails that were now making Luke's ears ache. Even the ones in the group who were fathers themselves had no luck. "Here, I'll hold it again," Luke said, reaching for his little buddy.

The crying instantly stopped, and the entire crew gaped at him in shock.

"I think he likes you…or she…" the captain said.

Luke shrugged. "I have no idea why. I've never really held a baby before."

He had thoughts about parenthood—someday, when everything in his life was in order and ready for him to think about getting married and having kids. Luke didn't live near his sister, so he hadn't held his nieces and nephews much when they were growing up. When Sam had offered him a chance to hold his newborn, Luke declined. He hadn't wanted to spread any germs to the little one. That's what he'd told everyone, at least. The real reason was that he'd thought that holding a baby might remind him that he felt called to be a father, but it just hadn't happened yet. Being around babies too much made him ache for something he did not have—a wife and kids of his own.

This baby, however, had needed him, so he picked it up without thought. And it seemed that the child wasn't about to let him go for a while. Luke attempted to hand the bundle off to the EMT when the ambulance backed out of the station, but the fussing began again.

"I think you'd better head to the hospital with them. The baby has attached itself to you," Sam said. "My wife said that it can happen in the few minutes after a drop-off because you are the person who is there for them during a traumatic time, like being separated from their mother."

Sam's wife, Fiona, was a social worker who worked with small children, so Luke trusted her on these matters. "Will she be the one that comes for the baby at the hospital?"

He would feel a little better if a friend were the one to make sure the baby went to a safe and stable home.

"No, she still has a week left of maternity leave, but I will have her call her boss and ask for the best social worker to respond," Sam said, his thumb brushing over the baby's cheek. Luke glanced around the group of firefighters crowded around them. It seemed they all had become attached to the little one.

"Tell her thanks from us." Luke gave his friend a nod before climbing into the back of the ambulance. The EMT, Maggie, held the baby while he strapped himself in. He tried to soothe its cries, which began when they were separated.

"You are going to have to let someone else hold you, little squirt. I can't be a baby carrier all night long," Luke said when he took the child back, wiping tears from its small face.

Maggie laughed. "Well, you might just be tonight. You're pretty good at that. I'm surprised that you're not a father already."

He shrugged. "I would love to be one someday. I'm just waiting for the right woman to come along."

Maggie chuckled. "Good luck with that. I was waiting for my ideal man, and my husband came around and surprised me by being someone completely outside of my expectations."

Luke didn't have the heart to tell her he had planned out his life exactly how he wanted it, and he would not be making any compromises. There was nothing wrong with knowing what you wanted. But finding the perfect woman to fit into his detailed plans had proved difficult, and he would not give in to the demands from his friends and family that he loosen up his requirements. God was in control, not them. Luke looked down at the little bundle in his arms. Maybe someday, God would bless him with a baby as cute as this. Or two. One boy and one girl. That was the goal.

Once they got to the hospital, the baby screamed every

time the nurses and doctors tried to examine him. They managed to tell him it was a little boy, though, and it seemed he wanted Luke to stay by his side, because the racket stopped whenever he was in the firefighter's arms.

"I don't mind," Luke told the nurse, who suggested they let the little one cry it out. "I've got nowhere to be."

His captain had texted him to say that he could spend the rest of his shift at the hospital, so he would make sure to personally hand this baby over to the social worker, or even the foster parent.

After the baby was examined and determined healthy, a volunteer led Luke to a rocking chair in a hospital room. They gave him a bottle and taught him how to feed him. "It feels weird that you don't have a name," Luke whispered to the baby, who gurgled happily now that he was getting fed.

"The birth certificate the doctor just sent in says 'Baby Boy,' because whoever adopts him will give him an official name," the nurse said.

Still, it felt weird that the baby could go weeks or months without any kind of name. "So what do you call babies who are in this situation?"

She shrugged. "Usually someone on staff picks a name, or the social worker does. Or the foster parents who take care of them until they find an adoptive home will call them something. Until then, they usually go by Baby Doe."

Luke cringed at that. It sounded like the baby was a victim in some sort of crime documentary. "The little guy should have a name," he asserted.

There was a knock on the door, and two women entered, smiling at him. "Why don't you name him?" one of them said.

She wore a business suit, her hair tightly pulled back

into a bun, and had a laptop and a small document folder clutched to her chest. The other woman looked like she had just rolled out of bed. Her light brown hair was up in a messy bun, and she wore sweatpants and a T-shirt that looked like it served as an apron with the number of stains on it.

She smiled at Luke and stepped forward to the little bundle in his arms. He had to lean over a bit because the woman was so much shorter than him. She ran a finger along the baby's cheek gently, then gave him a little boop on the nose. "Yeah, I think you should be the one to figure out what we should call this little squirt since he's so attached to you."

Though she had an unkempt appearance, Luke was immediately set at ease by the warmth in the woman's brown eyes and the smile that filled her whole face. It had him returning the grin instantly. "I've never named anyone before. I'll have to think about it."

The woman in the suit stepped forward and held out her hand. "Luke, my name is Sierra. I'm Fiona Tiernan's boss."

The social worker, already here to collect the baby. Sadness settled in Luke's gut. He wasn't ready to say goodbye. Besides, he needed more time to give the little guy a name.

"He cries when someone else holds him," Luke blurted out. Maybe they would take more time to ease the baby—and him—into the upcoming transition.

The unnamed woman standing next to him laughed. "So I've heard. But I've dealt with my share of crying babies before."

Luke arched an eyebrow at the strange person, who had yet to be introduced. Who was this short and wild-looking woman? Sierra cleared her throat and answered for him.

"This is Tessa Duncan. She's our emergency foster placement. She has a large home for plenty of kids who need care, and happens to have an infant bed open right now."

He studied the smiling woman and wondered if he could trust her with the little bundle he had become so attached to. Judging by the food stains all over her shirt, she could barely handle a meal, let alone a baby. "I'm sorry your night's sleep was interrupted."

Maybe his expression was a little too judgmental, because Tessa bit her lip as she looked down at her outfit. "Yeah, sorry, I just rolled out of bed. This kind of thing happens more often than you think, and I've found it's better to get here quickly than put too much time into looking put together at such an hour. I'd have to do a thorough search to find a shirt that the kids haven't decorated at dinner or snack time."

Tessa giggled when she said it, before pointing to his fire department–issued shirt and pants. "Some of us don't have government-issued uniforms to wear in a crisis."

He winced, knowing he had come off as a jerk. In his defense, it was the middle of the night and he was running on no caffeine. The baby's arrival had interrupted the fresh pot of coffee he was brewing. Luke wasn't qualified for normal human conversation at this point.

Luke apologized for his rudeness, and both women just waved it away, noting that none of them were at their best at this hour. Once again, he felt sorry for Tessa, who looked exhausted. "I was covering the overnight shift at the station and was already awake. I could have stayed with him until a decent time of day."

The women exchanged a glance and laughed. He didn't

know what was so funny, but the baby cooed against his chest, halting the frown that was brewing.

"At least half of our emergency placements happen in the middle of the night, so this was nothing new," Sierra said. "But you're right—I do hate making calls in the wee hours to our hardworking foster parents."

Tessa sighed and gave the social worker a side hug. "Don't start with all the guilty feelings. I wouldn't live this life if I wasn't called to it, even with all the ups and the downs. I had a bad date last night, so I wasn't sleeping well anyway."

The ladies seemed content to chat while Luke bounced the baby and tried to think of a good name for him.

Sierra cringed at the date news. "Another setup by the ladies across the street?"

Tessa nodded. "Yeah, and who am I to give up a free opportunity for babysitting beyond them just covering emergency calls like these. Even if it was a bad date, it was nice to get a break from all the wild ones running around my house."

"You don't get enough breaks, in my opinion," Sierra said with a sigh.

Luke clutched the baby close to him. Should he really pass his charge onto someone who didn't seem to like caring for children and needed a break from them? This wouldn't do at all. "Are you sure he should go home with her?"

Tessa couldn't help but smile at how tightly the man held the baby to his chest. The firefighter may not be too experienced with infants, but his protective instincts had certainly kicked in. She had to admire it—otherwise, she would be insulted by him implying she wasn't capable of caring for the baby. *Always look for the positive*, she told herself often.

"You don't have to worry about him. He will be in the best of hands," Tessa promised. "I have ten foster placements right now, and the older ones will be fighting for turns to be holding him. Not to mention all the volunteers who love to dote on babies."

Luke narrowed his eyes at her. "If you have so many foster kids, will you have the time to take care of one so little?" he asked, his voice laced with concern.

She wanted to roll her eyes at the question, but she gave him the benefit of the doubt. This man didn't know her, so he had no clue how often she took care of babies. "My home is a hybrid sort of group home with the foster system, the first of its kind. I provide homelike care instead of institutional, but I have volunteers who come in when they can and provide additional support."

Luke's brows furrowed in confusion. "I thought the state already had group homes."

Sierra nodded. "They do, but mostly for older kids. And they are more structured than the one Tessa has. Hers came out of necessity. We have so many kids in care and not enough places for the younger ones, especially emergency placements."

It had been her dream project when Tessa had bought the old Victorian at the heart of town with every last scrap of her savings she had put away through the years. She wanted to turn the home, which had been a hotel back in the late 1800s, into a haven for kids who needed a place to rest their heads and be loved before they found a more long-term place to stay. The only problem was that the upkeep of the old house was expensive. And she had more repairs to make on the house than she had time or money for. If she didn't meet all the safety requirements, however, her foster kids wouldn't have a safe home to go to when they needed it. She could not get shut down.

Tessa took a deep breath. That was a problem for another day. Right now, there was a little one right here that she could help. *One thing at a time*, she told herself.

"Can I hold him?" Tessa asked. "I would love to meet little…"

She left the question open, hoping the firefighter would come up with a name. The man cringed. "Okay, I'll think of something while you hold him as he screams," he said.

Tessa chuckled. "I will see if I can soothe him."

She held the baby in her arms and sang the song her own foster mother had crooned to her when she was young and in the state's care. "He's got the whole world in His hands…"

The Sunday school tune calmed all her new kids, and this one was no exception. The small boy stopped crying immediately. Luke's mouth dropped. "No one has been able to do that."

Tessa grinned at him. "Well, I guess he likes the both of us. You're a natural with him, by the way."

She took a moment to study him. The tall firefighter—he had at least a foot of height over her—looked polished in appearance, despite the late hour. His blond hair was in a classic gentleman's cut and perfectly in place. His uniform bore no wrinkles and was tucked perfectly into place. The only thing that was offbeat about him was a slight crookedness in his nose. She wondered if he had broken it while playing baseball as a kid or if it had happened on the job.

Her perusal was interrupted when Luke just shrugged

away her compliment on his baby handling. "I had the best example growing up with my dad. He was great with me and my sister."

She would have to take his word for it. In her experience, fathers were not all they were praised to be. "And your mom?"

A flash of pain crossed Luke's face. "She passed away when I was a kid."

Tessa closed her eyes. The last thing she wanted to do was bring up bad memories. "I'm so sorry. That must have been tough."

When she finally met his gaze again, his expression held nothing but warmth. "It's all right. It was a long time ago. But I think I have a name for this little guy."

"Oh yeah? What?" She was curious to know what she would call this little sweetheart for the short time he was in her care. While it hurt her heart to say goodbye to the kids who passed through her door, she knew that providing them love when they needed it most was an essential mission to which she had been called.

Luke puffed up his chest. "Thomas, after my dad."

Tessa smiled and looked down at the baby. "That's a grown-up name for such a little guy, but I like it. How about we call him Tommy for short?"

The baby sneezed, causing both of them to laugh. "I think he approves," Luke said. They were still smiling at each other and admiring the baby when Sierra came back into the room. Tessa blinked at her, not ever realizing the woman had gone anywhere. She had been so distracted by Tommy and Luke.

"I have all the paperwork done. You can take him home now if you'd like, Tessa," Sierra said.

Luke's shoulders slumped at that. It seemed the firefighter was having a hard time letting go. "Do you want to hold him one more time?" Tessa asked.

He held out his arms and took little Tommy, cradling the newborn's head exactly as he should. "I've only known him for a few hours, but this guy has already wrapped me around his finger. It's going to be hard to let him go."

Sierra reached out and caressed the soft hair on the baby's head. "He is a cutie pie. You know, I'm sure Tessa wouldn't mind if you came to visit him."

Tessa groaned inwardly. Her calendar was completely packed this week, and she had a to-do list that just wouldn't let up. How was she going to fit a guest on the agenda? "I don't know, my hands are full—"

Sierra's brows furrowed. "Don't you have enough volunteers this week? What about the repairs you have to get done? The state inspectors will be arriving soon, but I'm worried that you take on too much."

As she shifted on her feet nervously, Tessa tried to explain the situation to the case manager the best she could. She needed to prove that she could do it all. She could not fail those kids. "I'm fine. A few of my volunteers called in sick, so we're short this week. But you know I can always handle it."

Luke's eyebrow arched at their conversation. "You need some help? I would be happy to come by and lend a hand. I have the next two days off, so I could be at your disposal. Then I could see Tommy too."

Tessa gave him a small smile. He may be good with one baby, but how would the man handle a household full of wild kids? "I don't want to make you work on your time off."

Sierra clapped her hands in excitement. "He'll be fine.

This works out perfectly. I can mention to others that a fire-fighter is helping, and maybe more people will sign up too."

Well, there was a shortage of people willing to come sit with the kids and do household tasks, so Tessa didn't think she could say no to the offer. "Okay, if you would like to come, that would be great. But if you can only spare one day to help, I'd understand."

But judging from the way that the firefighter struggled to say goodbye to little Tommy, Tessa had a feeling he would be coming by more than once. She would find a way to put him to work. There was always plenty to do and few hands to do it. But she could never count on any help to last for long.

When Luke was finally able to pull himself away and head out the door, Tessa and Sierra prepared the baby for his next journey.

"I'm so glad you had an empty bed. The county is run-ning out of places for emergency placements lately," Si-erra said.

Tessa put Tommy in the baby carrier she'd brought with her. "Why is that? Are more kids coming into care?"

The case manager shook her head. "No, I don't think so, but there are a lot of cases of burnout among foster fami-lies. Which is why houses like yours will become more crucial in the future. Hopefully, you can help others open similar ones."

Tessa fidgeted with a tendril of hair that had fallen out of her messy bun. "It might be hard to find someone willing to put their life on hold and take care of ten kids at a time."

Sierra gave her a hug. "Did I ever tell you how much I appreciate you? And we need to figure out that life-on-hold thing. You need to ask for more volunteers and respite so you can have some more fun."

Tessa hoped the caseworker didn't think she was too overwhelmed. "Oh, I'm fine. I went out on a date last night."

Sierra cringed. "Yeah, but you said it didn't go well. What happened?"

"Most guys run for the door when they find out that I have ten kids at home. Which is fine. I knew what I was getting when I decided to open Harmony House."

Tessa lifted the baby carrier, and Sierra followed her to the elevator, moving ahead to hit the button. "But I'm hoping that someone will come along and join your mission."

"If not, I'm content to go at it alone. This is what I've been called to do," Tessa said. She meant that, truly, but she had to admit to herself that it got lonely sometimes. Fixing all the potential safety hazards in her house was the priority before her state inspection. Her love life could wait. Forever, if necessary.

Sierra walked her to her car and waited while she locked the carrier in the car seat. "At least you'll have a firefighter helping in your life's mission tomorrow. Maybe for the rest of the week too."

Tessa laughed. "I imagine he will take one look at the chaos at my house and run in the other direction."

She knew not much could bring a man who made a living running into fires to his knees, but she imagined her ten foster children might come close.

Chapter Two

Luke was dead on his feet by the time he finally drove out of the hospital's parking lot toward home. He briefly wondered if the baby would let Tessa have any sleep over the next few days. Judging by the woman's frazzled appearance, rest probably evaded her a lot. Taking care of a group home full of kids would do that to you, which was why he was firm in his plans to only have two kids, no more.

He and his sister had been enough company for each other growing up, and their dad had done an excellent job caring for them. He had never acted like they were too much to handle, even on the days when he had gotten into mischief with the other neighborhood boys.

Even though he wanted to crash the moment he got home, Luke was still thrilled to see his dad's truck in his driveway. His morning coffee with the guys down at the legion hall must have ended early.

Luke found Thomas Russell in his kitchen, on the floor, with his head under the sink.

"You fixed those pipes last week," he said, causing his dad to startle and almost hit his head on the cupboard doors.

"Yeah, well, I want to make sure it's tightened. The last thing you want is a leaky pipe under your sink."

Luke took a drink from a water bottle to hide his smile. Since his retirement, Dad "fixed" stuff every day in both his children's homes.

"You know I have a handyman business with some of the other firemen in our spare time," Luke said. "I know my way around kitchen plumbing."

His dad waved his hand as he got to his feet. "They should be paying you guys more so you don't have to do that. Besides, you need your rest. Looks like it was a rough night. You've got circles under your eyes."

Luke poured himself a bowl of cereal and handed the box to his dad, who also helped himself. "Yeah, we had an abandoned baby. I was the one there when he came in. I got to take him to the hospital and hold him until the foster mom could come and take care of him."

His dad scowled. "Who would abandon their own kid?"

Luke was so appreciative of his dad, who valued the well-being of his children above all else. "Someone that couldn't handle the responsibility, I guess."

That angered the older man even further. "Well, that's ridiculous. When you bring a kid into the world, you have to step up and take responsibility. I thought I wouldn't be able to handle it when your mom died, but I gave it my all and you turned out great."

He had a point, but Luke knew that every situation wasn't black and white. "We don't know what this parent was going through. We shouldn't judge."

His dad's shoulders sank. "Yeah, I guess all we can do is pray for the parent and the child. I'll add them to the list."

His dad kept a daily prayer list and mailed it out to his friends each week. The group of seniors were famous in this town for their dedication to praying for people by name.

"Yeah, little Tommy could use all the prayers he can get. He went to a foster home, and they will try to find someone to adopt him," Luke explained.

"Tommy, huh? Now I like the kid even more."

Luke laughed. "Yeah, well, since the baby took a liking to me, they let me name him. So I named him after you. There's no better example of a man to me, so I thought I would give him a good start in life."

Tears formed in his dad's eyes. "I don't even know what to say to that. Thank you, son. I did my best."

Luke nodded. "Your best was more than enough. I only hope the little guy gets a dad just like you."

The elder Thomas raised an eyebrow at that. "You seem to be pretty attached to this baby, even though you only spent a little time with him."

Luke thought about how Tommy had cried whenever anyone else held him. "I think we got attached to each other. I don't know, something about being there for him when he was all alone connected us somehow."

His dad smiled. "Well, I hope they give you an update on when he gets a family of his own."

Luke put his cereal in the bowl before turning back to his dad. "I'm going to stick around him for a while, just to make sure he's okay. I'm volunteering at the foster home he's at tomorrow. The lady there has a lot of kids and needs all the hands on deck that she can get."

That earned him a full belly laugh from his father. "You're going to help at a place where there are a bunch of children?"

What was he implying? "Yeah, you don't think I can handle it? I am a firefighter, after all."

His dad waved a hand to his neat and orderly home he'd

set up for himself. "Maybe I did a disservice running our home when you were growing up like I was still in the military, but it was the only way I knew how to do it."

While the way they had been raised was not traditional, Luke had nothing but good things to say about it. "What's wrong with that?"

The older man cleared his throat. "Well, your sister was always the independent one. She completely did things her own way when she became an adult. But you took everything I had taught you and rolled with it. Your life is so planned and organized, I'm worried you don't have the capacity for any surprises that life may throw your way."

Luke snorted. "I'm a firefighter. Surprise literally comes with the job."

His dad shrugged. "Yeah, but you have training and an exact manual you had to memorize on how to handle situations. Your gear has to be sorted and stored a certain way. The job suits that part of you."

Luke understood where his dad was coming from, but if his life wasn't broken, he shouldn't bother fixing it. "I think that having everything in order works well. I've worked hard to get to this point, where I can have a house and be ready to fill it with my family someday soon. I just have to find the right woman."

That earned him a chuckle. "And I'm sure you're looking for someone who is neat, organized and wants the same exact number of kids as you do."

He nodded. "Yeah, two kids to keep each other company. In a perfect world, a boy and a girl."

His dad gave him an affectionate slap on the back before putting his tools away. "You can't control the world—God does. And you certainly can't make it perfect."

Luke laughed. "Thanks for the vote of confidence, Dad."

"Well, I can't wait to be there when you learn that lesson," his father said before heading out the door with his toolbox.

Luke crashed headfirst into relaxation mode, spending the rest of his day lounging around before going to bed early. He was well rested when he got up early the next morning to follow the directions Sierra had called him with to Tessa's group home. When he pulled up to the curb, he could already see it was completely different from his own house.

The lawn needed to be mowed; he made a mental note maybe to do that later. But first, someone would have to pick up the toys that were left all over the front yard. A few bikes were tipped over in the driveway, as if they had been abandoned in a hurry.

There were cracks in the front sidewalk, and the porch could probably use a paint job. But the safety rails looked strong and sure, Luke acknowledged. Shouts and laughter on the other side of the door made him pause before knocking. Through the window, he could see two boys using sticks to fight like swords while jumping up and down on the couch. They also wore capes that looked like they were made of bed sheets.

"You will never take me alive," one boy yelled.

"You're gonna walk the plank when I win," responded the other.

Taking a deep breath, he raised his hand to knock, but another voice sounded out, "Miss Tessa! Someone stole the hairbrush, and I look awful!"

"You always look that way," came a singsong reply from another little girl.

He recognized Tessa's voice in the din, but it was too soft for him to make out the words. Hopefully, she was doing something to rein these children in. The house sounded like chaos, and for a moment, he wondered if his dad was right—he wasn't prepared to enter this wild kingdom that Tessa ran.

The decision was made for him when the door swung open, and a little boy, probably no more than seven or eight years old, stood there, eyeing him with suspicion. He folded his arms and leaned against the doorway, clearly trying to protect the home from any danger that Luke might present. He had to respect the kid for his bravado when faced with a stranger.

"What do you want?" the kid asked.

"Zack, that's not nice! We don't speak to people that way, especially ones that come to volunteer to help," Tessa's voice came from behind him.

Luke couldn't help the smile that formed on his face when she came into view. She was wearing different clothes from yesterday's, and her socks were mismatched, but she had the same sunny mannerisms that had put him at ease last night. "Hi, I'm reporting for duty."

Inwardly, he cringed at the military terms. Maybe his dad's upbringing really did have a bigger impact on him than he'd previously recognized. He was just now noticing these little things since his dad had brought it up. He tightened his shoulders. There was nothing wrong with being that way, though, and he would show everyone that an orderly life was a comfortable one.

Tessa smiled at him as she ushered him in the door. "Well, there is plenty to do. I'm sorry the baby is sleeping, but you can help make breakfast if you'd like."

Zack narrowed his eyes. "You're helping us today? Where's Mrs. Thompson?"

Tessa threaded her fingers through the boy's hair. "She had a doctor's appointment, remember? She told you that she would be back later this week, though."

The little boy huffed. "She made the best pancakes. Do you use blueberries in yours?"

Luke put his hand on his chin thoughtfully, trying to hide his smile. "Yeah, I've been known to make some blueberry pancakes in my day, but have you tried them with chocolate chips?"

Zack hopped up and down. "No, but that sounds amazing!"

He was shouting at the end there, and Luke cringed when Tessa shushed him. "You don't want to wake the baby, bud. Mr. Luke wants to see little Tommy, but probably not when he's cranky and tired."

It seemed there was already enough noise in the house to keep anyone awake, but he kept that thought to himself. Luke practically bounced with his own excitement at the prospect of seeing the baby again. "I'm not worried about a grumpy baby. Remember, he doesn't cry much for me."

Tessa giggled. "Well, we will have to see if that still applies when he's hungry and sleepy."

Without another look at Luke, she steered Zack toward the back of the house, which he presumed was where the kitchen was. He didn't know if he was supposed to follow, so he just stood there awkwardly for a moment, catching his bearings. The room wasn't neat and organized like his place: there were kids' drawings taped to the wall, shoes tossed haphazardly by the door, and more throw pillows and blankets than any family could possibly need. Another wall was covered with school pictures of probably fifty different kids.

Were these all the children whom Tessa had helped through the years? It was awe-inspiring. Even more determined to offer her all the help he could, Luke started organizing the shoes by the door. He had them all lined up in rows within a few minutes, making a note on his phone to order a shoe rack for her.

"What are you doing?"

He turned to see Tessa standing in the hallway, a bemused smile on her face. He got to his feet. "I came here to help, so I'm helping."

She shook her head. "While I appreciate the way the shoes look, I can promise you they will only last about ten minutes like that, at most. I have to do things by priority around here. And right now that's breakfast. I think you promised someone chocolate chip pancakes. It's a good thing I got all the ingredients for those during my last grocery run. Can you make those while I get the rest of the big kids out of bed and ready for school? I usually let the littles sleep as long as I can."

Luke had no idea how she managed all this chaos without any sort of order or system in place, but this wasn't his house, so he had to play by her rules. He would address the shoe situation later. There had to be a way to teach these kids not to just leave them in piles on the floor.

He followed her directions to the kitchen, nervous about what he might find there. If the living room was that cluttered, he knew the kitchen was bound to be worse. He was not wrong. It was lived in and eclectic, yet still clean and efficient. There seemed to be things taking up space in every spot on the counter, but there were no dirty dishes or spilled food around. "Okay, bud, pancakes coming right up, but you've gotta help me clear a space so I can mix them up."

Zack had laid out the ingredients on the kitchen island, which was clutter free. "Why? We can just make them here."

Luke shook his head. "Yeah, but it's hard for me to focus with all this stuff around."

Zack gave him a serious look before nodding. "I get it. You have ADHD like me. I have to take medicine every morning and sit close to the teacher and try not to look at distractions on the wall."

He had been the same in school, but he had never gotten any sort of diagnosis for it. Back then, he was just a troublemaker. Luke glanced at the clock. He probably didn't have a lot of time for a full kitchen-organization project. The others would be down for food soon.

"Okay, I'm going to put in all the ingredients, and while you mix them up, I'm going to put all these food boxes on the counter away."

Zack laughed. "You're going to make Miss Tessa mad."

Who would be mad about a little bit of organization? "Let me worry about her," he said after dumping the last ingredients into the big bowl. "You just come over here and put your strongest mixing arm to work."

He laughed when the little boy flexed both his muscles before finally deciding on his right hand to grab the spoon. Zack stirred with all his might as Luke picked up a handful of food packages that were lined up on the counter and put them in the pantry. He winced after noticing the door was being held up by only one hinge. It looked like this house may be in the need of a few repairs.

Luke made a mental note to grab a screwdriver from

his emergency tool kit in his car before he left. Shaking the thought from his head, he returned to his project of arranging the food boxes in the pantry by height, then width.

"There, perfect. Now she'll be able to find them better, and the kids will be able to see what snacks they have," Luke murmured to himself.

"I think it's all mixed," Zack called from the other room. Luke hurried out and checked his work, stirring the pancake batter a bit more to catch a clump of dry mix that had been missed by his young assistant.

"This looks great. Now we just have to add the chocolate chips and get them in the pan."

Luke let Zack pour the chips in and stir while he got things going on the stove, and soon enough, the smell of pancakes filled the entire house. Kids started trickling in, taking seats at the table, in various states of being ready for school. One girl looked like she was still asleep, laying her head down on the table the moment she sat down.

"That's Jessie. She is not a morning person, so it's best not to even talk to her until after lunch," Zack said in a serious tone. "That's River, Micah, MacKenzie and Neveah. The rest of the kids who live here are too little to go to school."

Luke wondered how many people actually lived in this house and where Tessa put them all. The wild chaos was so completely different from the calm and neatness of his own place that it made his head spin.

"Everyone eating? Great," Tessa said as she entered the room, carrying baby Tommy. "Can you hold him while I get the rest of the food?"

She passed the bundled boy off before Luke barely had time to react, but he was able to recover enough in time to support the baby's head properly. Luke looked down at his little buddy, happy to see him safe and sound after their traumatic meeting. "Hey there, Tommy. Did you miss me?"

Tessa smiled at him. "He hasn't cried a ton, the sweet boy, but I think the times when he did, it meant he was missing you."

Luke smirked. "For sure, and not because he was hungry or tired."

"Of course not," Tessa said with a wink. She reached out and swept her hands along the counter. "Where are the boxes of food that were here?"

He puffed out his chest. "I took some time while making breakfast to put it all away for you and organize your pantry."

Tessa heaved a sigh and pinched the bridge of her nose. "You didn't need to do that."

Luke nuzzled the fine hairs on Tommy's head with his nose. The baby gurgled back at him. He really was cute. Luke wanted to support Tessa all he could because she gave up so much of herself to take care of these kiddos, even if chaos reigned supreme around here. He wondered how many other little ones like Tommy had come through her door. "I know I didn't have to, but I wanted to be of help."

She cringed. "I really wish you hadn't done that, even if your motives were pure."

Luke's jaw dropped at the barely restrained annoyance in her expression. She wasn't happy about his hard work. "Did I do something wrong?"

That couldn't be the case. Organizing made everything better. She would be able to take care of the kids much more efficiently if all items had a place.

Tessa grabbed the boxes he had carefully put away and

put them back on the counter. "Some of the kids have allergies. And some only eat certain things. I have them out on the counter in certain spots so I can make sure I pay attention to giving them the right food."

He furrowed his brow at that. "Can't you organize them like that in the pantry?"

She shrugged. "It's easier to access them quickly on the counter. I have a system."

Luke was skeptical that such an untidy system would work, but he let it be for now. This was her house, and he was just here to volunteer for a few days while he could see the baby. No use making waves. "Well, if you don't want my organizational help, what can I do for you instead?"

He noticed other little things here and there he could fix if he had the time. The handle was coming off the cupboard in the kitchen. Hinges on the doors were loose. The baseboards needed to be repainted. There were plenty of items he could add to his to-do list while volunteering.

But the head of Harmony House had other plans for him. Tessa held up a loaf of bread. "How are you at making PB&Js? I could use help packing their lunches while I finish getting them ready. After they are gone, then we can talk about what needs to be done around here."

I guess it's kitchen duty for me today, Luke thought as he put little Tommy down in the portable crib in the dining room and started to make sandwiches. And that had been his chore at the fire station last week too. Maybe God knew that he needed the practice or something.

Tessa breezed by him to braid the hair of one of the little girls while drilling the other on her spelling words for the week. It amazed Luke at how light on her feet she was. She seemed to always be in motion yet carried herself with an ease that never revealed how chaotic her life was. Luke wondered how that was possible. He was barely able to contain his yawns while putting together all the lunches that were needed.

"You exhausted already? Because our day is just getting started," Tessa said after they got all the kids out the door and to the bus stop at the end of her driveway. "Now it's time to wake up the toddlers, who make the older kids seem practically perfect."

Luke groaned. This morning had been wild so far, and he still had the whole day ahead of him. Seeing baby Tommy was worth it, but he had a feeling he would be fighting the urge to flee many more times. But his dad hadn't raised a quitter. He would be the best volunteer Tessa ever had.

"Let's do this."

Within a few minutes, the stampede of cranky toddlers hungry for breakfast began.

Chapter Three

"What do I do?" Luke asked as two angry little ones were screaming beneath him, their arms in the air, begging to be held. Tessa held back a laugh at the look of sheer terror in his eyes. *He really is a fish out of water here*, she thought. *But at least he is trying.*

"Just jump in anywhere and do what you can to keep them calm while I get their breakfast together," Tessa said.

He edged closer to her. "Why don't you watch them while I make breakfast?"

Tessa bit her lip. It was really hard not to smile, since his leg was now wrapped with two-year-old limbs. "Nonsense. You made breakfast and lunch for the other kids. I've got this. You just play for a while. I know the exact portions they need, so it will be easier for me to do it."

Luke gave her another panicked look before he picked up a ball and tossed it across the room. "Go get it! Fetch!"

She could no longer hold it back—a big belly laugh burst out of her. "They aren't dogs."

He shrugged and gestured to the kids toddling after the ball. "It worked, didn't it?"

She was still giggling as she chopped up a banana into little pieces and added Cheerios to the children's plates. She scrambled some eggs and added a small amount of those to their meals as well. When she returned to the family room, Luke was holding baby Tommy and each of the little ones was lined up for a turn to see the baby. "They think he's awesome too," Luke said when he spotted her shaking her head at the scene.

"You're getting awfully attached to him," Tessa noted. It wasn't a bad thing to love the kids her in care, but as foster placements, they were only a temporary part of their lives.

Luke shrugged. "I don't know if it's because I was just the only one there for him when his mother left him in that baby box or something about him in particular, but I feel this connection with him. I want to make sure he gets the very best start in life."

Tessa smiled. "You know, I'm a single foster parent. They allow those, and single adoptive parents. Maybe if you are that attached to him, you could apply to be a more permanent part of his life."

The color drained from Luke's face. "Oh, um, I don't think I would do that. I have my plans for the future, and I'm definitely waiting until I'm married to have any kids."

She felt her jaw tighten. "Single parents can do a lot in this world. They pour out every piece of themselves for their kids."

Luke had the wisdom to look apologetic. "I'm sorry, I didn't mean to imply that you weren't an exceptional single foster parent. I'm just saying that it's not for me. Besides, I don't think they would approve of me. I'm a firefighter with weird hours, and I can get called out at a moment's notice. They may not think that is a stable enough environment for a kid. Hence the need for a wife."

Tessa understood. The foster care and adoption calling

wasn't for everyone. "Well, in that case, you are going to have to learn the fine balance of giving little Tommy all the love and support he needs right now but be able to let him go when the time comes."

An anguished expression crossed his face so quickly that she would have missed it if she wasn't paying close attention to him. He really did care for the baby. "So I need to be attached but not too attached?"

Tessa nodded, and he frowned. "How do you do it all the time? Love these kids and then send them off back to their birth parents or into a family who will be a long-term foster or adoption situation?"

It is so hard, and I cry about it sometimes, she thought, but she didn't want to show that weakness to him. "I just remember that they are going to the situation that is best for them, and I'm here to help them when they need me the most. If they don't need me anymore, that's a good thing."

But it was still so hard to let them go. Luke studied her for a moment before nodding and returning his attention back to Tommy. She let him enjoy time with the little guy while she fed the toddlers. After finding a baby carrier by the door, Luke jumped in to help with play time. He waved her off to go do something else while he entertained the kids.

"Are you sure you can handle this?" she asked.

Luke gave her a wink. "I think my initial fear wore off. I've got these guys. You go do what you have to do."

Tessa didn't need to be told twice. She hurried to clean up for the day; it was a rare occurrence that she got the chance to do that before naptime. Then she caught up on her email and double-checked her schedule for some of the work-from-home assignments she had taken on for the week.

She was so distracted by the computer that it took her a while to notice how quiet the house had become.

Too quiet.

One lesson she had learned in childcare was that silence was a dangerous thing. Who knew what kids were getting up to when they weren't being loud and telegraphing all their shenanigans to the world? With visions of Luke being tied up and overrun by a gang of toddlers, Tessa hurried down the stairs.

She gasped at the sight when she entered the playroom. Not only was Luke not overwhelmed by children, but he also had them completely under control. Her two- to three-year-old charges were marching in time as he called out commands.

"We playing army," little MacKenzie shouted in garbled toddler-speak.

Tessa hid her grin. Luke had found a way to entertain the kids with his overly organized personality style. She wondered if he had served in the military in the past. It made sense, based on what she was seeing.

"Were you in the army?" she asked as he got the kids to line up single file to march toward their rooms for naptime.

He shook his head. "No, my dad was, though. This was how he got me to clean my room and brush my teeth. By making it a very serious military matter."

Tessa laughed. "Well, I'm glad these kiddos are so dedicated to doing their duty for their country."

Luke helped her put them all down for a nap. Then he completed every task she asked of him throughout the day. Tessa had expected him to skip out on the hard stuff, but the firefighter bravely battled the laundry piles and dirty dishes like a pro. Toward the end of the day, he even helped the older kids with their homework. Maybe this man really was built as tough as his job made him appear to be.

"I like him," third grader Bailey whispered to Tessa in the kitchen after Luke assisted her through math. "Can we keep him?"

Tessa laughed and tousled the girl's hair. "Only for a couple of days. Do you want to make some cookies?"

She had a while before the youngest kids woke up from their afternoon nap. Tessa tried to time the naps to coincide with the end of the school day so she could focus some of her attention on the older kids. Usually, she sat with them and worked on homework at this time.

Bailey's eyes widened. "Really? We never get to do that!"

Seeing how excited the little girl was at getting one-on-one attention from her, Tessa felt a tug in her heart. Yet another reason to be grateful for Luke's presence here today.

"Tessa! I got all my spelling words right, so Luke is going to teach me how to throw a football," Zack said as he and the firefighter entered the room wearing matching grins.

She smiled back at them, happy this sweet boy got some attention from an adult as well. Maybe having a man around the house from time to time wasn't such a bad thing after all. "That sounds like so much fun, buddy. We'll have some cookies for you all when you're done."

"I hope they are chocolate chip—they're my favorite. Come on, kid. Let's toss the ball a little, and then maybe we can assemble those bookshelves in the box that is collecting dust in the playroom. I'm going to need your help. It's definitely a two-man job," Luke said.

"Yeah! I think the screwdriver is in the junk drawer,"

Zack said. The look of adoration for Luke the young boy held in his eyes made something catch in Tessa's throat.

Don't get too attached, Tessa reminded herself as the two went out the back door and Bailey chatted happily while getting out the ingredients. She didn't know if her warning was for her sweet foster kids, the firefighter or both.

Chapter Four

Luke knocked on Tessa's door bright and early the next morning, with coffee and doughnuts in hand. The kids squealed with delight when he entered the house with the box, but their foster mom just lifted an eyebrow.

He interjected before she could protest his breakfast plan. "I made sure they included some for the ones with allergies."

Luke held up several bags that each held doughnuts that were gluten free, dairy free, egg free and free from other allergens. "I paid attention," he declared proudly.

Tessa rewarded him with a huge grin that made him want to do even more around here. Her hair was falling out of its messy bun again—making him wonder if all mornings were chaotic around here.

She grabbed the doughnuts and started putting them on plates for the kids. "Thank you. I can't believe you remembered all that. Did your military upbringing include memory drills or something?"

He chuckled, thinking of all the times his father had quizzed him on his math tables. "Something like that. Tommy awake?"

She opened her mouth to answer him, but the newborn responded instead with a wail that made everyone wince.

"I've got him. You feed these munchkins," he said.

Luke followed the sound of the baby crying down a hallway to a room that held three cribs, two of which looked like they had been converted into toddler beds. Tommy's little limbs writhed with each wail.

"Hey, buddy, what's the matter?" Luke asked softly, scooping his favorite little guy out of the bed.

As per usual, the baby quieted down the moment he was in Luke's arms.

Tessa entered the room a few minutes later to a happy baby cooing and grabbing Luke's shirt. "You're just too good with him. And judging from the smile on your face, he's good for you too."

Luke just shrugged. "I don't know what it is about this kid. Ever since I laid eyes on him, I've felt connected to him."

Tessa reached out and ran her fingers along the baby's fine curls. "The feeling is mutual. He doesn't when I hold him, but he's much happier with you. I wonder what he'll be like with his future foster or adoptive parents."

Luke's heart ached at the thought of others caring for him, but he knew it was for the best. "I know this little guy has the perfect home waiting for him somewhere. He will have parents that also make him happy."

Tessa kept looking between him and the baby. He knew what she was going to say before she opened her mouth. "You know I stand by what I said earlier …you'd be a good foster parent."

A surge of panic swelled within Luke that she wasn't letting this topic go. That chaotic lifestyle was definitely not part of his regimented plan. He was distracted from his thoughts when a little whimper sounded from Tommy.

Luke's eyes shot up and met Tessa's. "What's the matter with him?"

She giggled. "Most babies want one of two things after their nap… I'm guessing he's hungry. I'm going to go warm up a bottle for him."

When she left the room, Luke stared down at the baby in his arms, not complaining at all about more time with the little guy.

"I told your namesake, my dad, about you. He really wants to meet you someday. Maybe if you get a nice family, they will still let you come down to the fire station to visit me from time to time," he whispered to Tommy.

The baby's only response was to wiggle in his arms. *Clearly hungry and not up for conversation*, Luke thought with a chuckle. He imagined how fun it would be to have little Tommy come down to the station every once in a while so they could watch him grow up.

But that was only if he went to a family that lived nearby. And one that was willing to still let Luke see him after the adoption.

"Why are you frowning so much? Because he's finally fussing in your presence?"

Luke shook his head. "I'm just woolgathering. Besides, my little guy wouldn't fuss for me, other than to tell me he was hungry that one time. He's just wiggly."

Tessa tilted her head to study the pair. "I think that hunger might be what's going on with him now. Do you want to feed him? Even though he's fussy, I have a feeling that someone else holding him when he's hangry will just make it worse."

Luke nodded and sang a song to Tommy as Tessa hurried to prepare the bottle. When he was finally done with his third chorus of "Twinkle, Twinkle, Little Star," he looked up to see Tessa leaning against the doorframe, a tender smile on her face. He felt his cheeks warm.

"Don't stop on my account. You have a lovely voice," she teased, handing over the bottle. Her wild hair was falling into her face as she leaned over to give Tommy a kiss on the forehead. "Dinner and a show, little man. Only a few days old and already living your best life."

Luke chuckled. "Well, technically, breakfast and a show, but I live to serve."

Tessa flashed him a grin, and he couldn't help but notice that she was actually quite pretty now that he wasn't studying her under hospital lights. Luke even found her wild bun quite endearing.

He cleared his throat, needing to focus on the task at hand. "Um, I guess I better feed him."

She took a step back from them and nodded. "I've got to get the older kids off to school. Don't forget to burp him."

And then it was just him and Tommy again. And while he loved time with his favorite little guy, the room felt a little bit emptier without Tessa's company.

Fifteen minutes later, Tessa had the toddlers glued to their favorite TV show while she cleaned up the breakfast mess. She needed to invest in some orthopedic shoes from the amount of time she spent on her feet every day, running around, being a mom. But she wouldn't trade her life for anything.

Tessa was distracted from her thoughts by the sound of the phone buzzing on her countertop and the kids yelling at the top of their lungs to let her know. She bit her lip to keep from laughing as she answered.

The half smile dropped from her face, however, when Sierra's normally cheerful voice sounded tight with stress on the other end of the line.

"What's wrong?" Tessa asked right away, not wanting to waste time with small talk.

Sierra sighed. "Do you have a minute?"

Tessa sank onto one of the stools by the kitchen counter. Sierra's tone was ominous…not like the one she used when asking her to take another placement, but like the one she used when another shoe was about to drop.

"So…the state has taken a huge interest in your group home," Sierra started. "You know there are not a lot of homes like this for younger kids. They mostly have them for teens. They are skeptical that so many kids in one place would be an ideal home for them. They don't want to return to the orphanages of old."

Tessa held back a groan. This was an argument she had all the time with well-meaning people who did not understand her mission. Her home was a safe haven for kids who needed an emergency place to stay for a short time. It wasn't meant to be a permanent place. But Tessa firmly believed that just because something was temporary didn't mean it couldn't feel like a real home.

"They just don't get it. But they will," she said. She was determined to prove that places like this were a necessity.

Sierra gave a hum in agreement. "Yeah, well, because of their interest, they want to make sure all your *i*'s are dotted and your *t*'s are crossed. If they are going to invest in similar projects long term, they want to make sure it's running smoothly here."

Tessa gritted her teeth. She hated always having to prove herself. She ran a good program, but this house was chaotic most of the time. Like a real family. They had messes and boo-boos and the general wildness that came with many children. Well-cared-for children.

"So what does this all mean?" She needed to know what to expect so that she could get to work as soon as possible.

"It means they're coming for an inspection one month from today," Sierra said, a hint of nervousness coloring her voice. "I know it's not much time, but…"

Tessa glanced around the house. The toys, the broken cupboards, the flour mess from pancakes this morning, the toilet that kept clogging… A pressure started building in her chest.

"A month? You couldn't ask for a bit longer?"

Sierra sighed. "I did. A month was a compromise after they originally tried for two weeks from now. I think you can do it."

Tessa was thankful that her case manager always believed in her and what she did here for the kiddos, but this might be an unreasonable expectation.

"You know this house is an old one. I mean, it's safe for the kids, but it's nothing that will impress a group of inspectors. I don't want them to get a bad impression and shut me down," Tessa said.

Sierra was quick to reassure her. "I'm not going to let that happen. There is such a need for this kind of program. I don't want to go back to the days when the foster homes were all full and the kids were sleeping on the floor in the office until we could find long-term placements for them."

Tessa shuddered at the thought of any of the kids in her care going through something like that when they were already traumatized by being separated from their parents.

"Well, I will just have to impress these inspectors so that

we can have more emergency group homes like this," Tessa said. She didn't care if it took her every waking minute of the next thirty days—she would prove that this dream of hers was a success.

"Atta girl. I know you can show them that. You have what it takes to not only make your place succeed but to teach others to do the same," Sierra said. "I'll come out and help when I can. And I'm sure that others in the community will be willing to come too."

Tessa snorted at that. Most of the volunteers, with the exception of Luke, were from the senior homes and veterans' halls. Not exactly the muscle she needed to get this place into shape. She shook away the thought. She wouldn't bring fear into this. She didn't have time for it. Tessa had two hands, and she was going to find a way fix this house up.

After she got off the phone, she sat there in silence, mentally making a list of all the things she had to do now.

"Are you okay?" Luke's voice came from behind Tessa, startling her. She almost fell off her seat until he reached out a firm hand on her shoulder to steady her. "Whoa, there, I didn't mean to scare you. It just seemed like you were thinking really hard about something. Maybe I can help?"

His other arm was wrapped around baby Tommy, holding him at his shoulder. Luke let go of Tessa and started putting soft pats on the baby's back. She couldn't believe he had just learned how to hold a baby properly and was already burping him. It seemed that Luke was a quick study. Tessa hoped she would have the same speed when fixing up the house this month.

"I'm fine," she said immediately, but then walked back the statement a bit, rubbing her temples to fight off the headache forming there. "You ever had a to-do list so long and overwhelming that you don't know where to start?"

Luke opened his mouth to speak, but she cut him off with a chuckle. "Never mind, I forgot who I was talking to. You're so regimented that you probably have to-do lists for your to-do lists," Tessa said.

They both cracked up but then quieted when little Tommy stirred at the noise. Tessa sat back in her chair with a smile, inviting him to sit at the kitchen table next to her. He did so very gently, careful not to wake the baby again as Tommy gave a little snore.

"I do make a lot of lists, but I know what you're talking about, though. Sometimes that happens when we get to a fire scene," Luke said. "There is so much going on that it's hard to figure out what to do first."

"So how to you get done what needs to be done in that moment? I mean, my problem is not as high pressure as a fire, but I'm definitely feeling the stress," Tessa said.

Luke gave her a smile. "By working together as a team and everyone doing their part to make sure it all gets handled."

Tessa's shoulders sank. "I don't really have a team."

"I don't know what's going on, but I can help," he volunteered quickly.

She arched a brow at that. "I thought you were just here to help with the baby and do a little bit of volunteering on the side."

He waved her off with his free hand. "Nonsense. As a fireman, it's my duty to assist where needed."

Tessa rolled her eyes. "I'm not sure that firemen assist with construction and home repairs."

At his prompting, she filled Luke in on the phone call

with Sierra and the impending visit from the state inspectors. "I promise you... I'm going to help you get everything done. I'll even ask around the church to see if anyone else can spare some time to come out. I think there are some college kids that will be heading to school soon, so we might as well take advantage of their last days of freedom for some manual labor."

He gave her a sly grin, but Tessa's stomach churned. It had been a long time since she had been in church. And all she remembered were the hours her foster parents spent trying to get her and the other children in their care to sit still.

"Why would they help me? I'm not even a member," she asked. "I mean... I believe in God, but I haven't really set aside much time for organized religion. I haven't had the time."

Tessa felt a twinge of guilt. She had heard the local church had a great Sunday school and Vacation Bible School program, but getting them all dressed and out the door by herself had seemed too daunting.

"You've had a lot on your plate, but I'm your friend now. And I'm going to let you in on a little secret," Luke said. "You don't have to be a member for us to help you."

She blinked at that. They had only known each other for a few days, but after being in the trenches with the kids, it did feel like they were forming a sort of friendship.

Still, they weren't close enough for this big of a favor... But could she afford to say no? "Are you sure?"

Luke stood and walked quietly to the living room and laid the sleeping baby into the bassinet she kept there. Tessa was amazed that the large fireman could move so gently. After his arms were free, he grabbed a notepad and pen from where she kept them in a drawer in the coffee table.

"How did you know those were there?"

He shrugged. "One of the kids begged me to draw them a picture of a dragon. For the record, that is not one of my life skills."

Tessa's lips turned up. She was amazed that he could make her smile despite the daunting task in front of her. "Oh yeah? Do I get to see this work of art?"

Luke shook his head. "No way. I burned that thing when I got home. I saved your eyes from torture."

They shared a laugh, and he handed her the notebook and pen. "Here, make a list of all the things that you need done to help this place run more smoothly, and I'll see what I can do."

She stared at the items in his hand before finally taking them. It usually felt so wrong to ask for help, but for some reason, with Luke, he made it seem easy.

"Okay, let's go room to room so we make sure we don't forget anything."

He rubbed his hands together. "See, now you're getting it. Making a plan to help make a plan. My kind of a good time."

She rolled her eyes at that, but her heart felt much lighter as she got to work on her task.

Chapter Five

Tessa couldn't believe when Sierra showed up the next day in her casual clothes, ready to work.

"I took a few days off," she said sheepishly. "I have so many PTO days that I've earned the right to be spontaneous and come to help you."

Tessa couldn't resist. She pulled the other woman in for a warm hug. "Thank you so much! You don't know how much this means to me!"

Sierra surprised her by running back out to her car and bringing in several cans of paint. "I got that yellow that you've been talking about. To make the toddler room more cheerful. If we are going to do an overhaul of everything, we might as well make sure it's just how you want it."

Tessa had only been thinking about the immediate needs of her home, not her dream list of what she wanted to do with it. "Maybe…if we have time."

Sierra put the cans in the closet nearest the front door. "Well, it can be our reward for everything else we get done. Now, I have my tool kit my dad gave me for my birthday. Where do you want me to get started?"

Tessa eyed the bright pink box in Sierra's hands. "It's a tool kit?"

"Well, a lady can be stylish and handy at the same time."

Tessa laughed and asked Sierra to get started on tightening all the kitchen cupboards with her.

"I heard through the grapevine that the church down the road is sending a group this weekend to lend a hand," Sierra said.

Tessa was amazed the news had traveled so fast since Luke had only mentioned it yesterday. The group was quick and kindhearted, both traits that would come in handy over the next month.

"Yeah, Luke decided to get the church involved. I can't believe he's so willing to help with all of this," Tessa said.

Sierra paused in her search for the right screwdriver. "Why not?"

Tessa shrugged. "I've been doing this all alone for so long and have never really asked for help."

Her friend grabbed the right screwdriver and pointed it at her. "You don't know how to ask for help, you mean."

Tessa couldn't help but agree. "I guess somewhere in my mind, it makes me feel like a failure if I have to get too much help. A few senior volunteers from time to time to watch the kids, sure, but I've always prided myself in being a strong, competent woman."

Sierra was silent for a moment, deep in thought as she started to tighten the screws on one of the lower cupboards. "You know I say this with all the love in my heart, right?"

"Uh…sure," Tessa said warily, knowing that she probably wasn't going to like what Sierra said next.

"But you have to remember your purpose in starting this place. About your mission to give these kids comfort at the time when they need it most. Asking for help doesn't make you a failure—it just shows that you put the needs of the kids above everything, even fear and pride."

Tessa knew she was right. If she had to keep this place open, she needed to be willing to let other people in. Which is why, a couple of days later, she let Luke and a big group from the church into the house with their tools and cleaning supplies. Since there were so many people on hand, Tessa decided to paint the toddlers' room after all.

Luke joined her, and they passed the day chatting as they applied the primer, along with the first coat of paint. Several people from the church had taken over childcare for the day, so it was a nice reprieve for Tessa as well, despite the ache in her muscles from the manual labor.

"Can I ask you a personal question?" Luke asked as they prepared to put on the second coat.

"I guess. I don't have a lot of secrets. You can't, when you have to go through the ringer to get approved as a foster mom," Tessa said with a laugh.

"That's what I was going to ask about. What made you want to do this? To qualify as a single foster mom and start a group home? It's amazing, but I don't think it's a common life goal for many young women," he said.

Tessa snorted. "Yeah, ringleader of my own personal circus did not come up on my career-day assessment test."

"So why did you choose this route?"

Tessa mulled over her answer for a moment, wondering how much of her past she should share with him. Something about Luke made him easy to talk to, but she never wanted to be someone who dumped all their trauma out in casual conversation.

"It's a long story. Tragic childhood and wanting to give back, basically," she explained.

Luke laid a hand on her arm. "Tess, I want to know. Really. If you're comfortable talking about it."

The earnest look in his eyes convinced her to open up to him. She stepped away from him and busied herself with painting the trim while she talked.

"Well, I don't remember my dad at all. He ran off when I was young, and then died. It was just my mom and me for years," Tessa said.

She closed her eyes for a moment, remembering how her mom smelled like vanilla and always gave her the warmest hugs. How they used to sing in the kitchen together and dance around the table on Taco Tuesdays.

"We were a great team, the pair of us. But then, when I was eight, she died in a car accident," Tessa said.

She jumped when Luke wrapped an arm around her shoulders. "I'm so sorry that happened to you, Tess. That must have been heart-wrenching."

Tessa let herself be pulled into a hug. It felt nice to have someone who cared. "Thanks. It was. But it was also a long time ago, and I've had time to heal and use the experience to help others. When it first happened, I bounced around from one scary emergency placement to the next. I was terrified and I just wanted to go home, even though I didn't really have one. Not anymore. I felt more like a package being shipped around than a person."

Luke nodded. "Okay, so your mission here makes a little more sense now."

Tessa continued, "Yeah, after I was in care for several years, I ended up in the care of a single foster mom. She was amazing."

Luke squeezed her hand. "Like you."

She shrugged. "That's my hope. Ronnie raised me as

her own. She didn't need anyone to help her raise all those kids. People gave her a lot of judgment back then for not getting married, to have someone share her life and ministry to foster kids, but we all got along just fine without a foster father."

And the kids in her home would, too, Tessa told herself.

Luke stepped back and bumped her shoulder. "Well, I was raised by a single dad after my mom passed away. He is amazing. I don't think it matters if a kid has a single mom or a single dad. What matters is the quality and the strength of the parent," he said. "And I think you have just the quality and strength that these kids need."

Tessa wiped a tear that had started running down her face. She'd had no idea how much she'd needed to hear something like that.

They got back to work shortly after that conversation, but Luke kept a close eye on Tessa for the rest of the afternoon. Their conversation had shaken her. He hadn't meant to bring up all those bad memories for her. But her life was so different from his; he had just been so curious as to how she'd gotten here.

Something in her story stuck out to him. Tessa seemed to need to prove to the world that she could do all this, without the help of a partner. His own father had succeeded, but it had taken a toll on him throughout the years.

There had been many times his father had worked extra hours to make sure there was food on the table and money for all the extra things they needed for school and home. There were times when his dad had looked sad, lonely or just plain exhausted.

But he never complained. Not once. And neither did

Tessa. But just because they were capable of doing something like this on their own, it didn't mean it was ideal.

He noted the dark circles under Tessa's eyes. Just how much was she taking on herself?

"How much rest do you get? I can't imagine you sleep for more than a few hours at night with the babies and the toddlers waking up and needing things," Luke said.

Tessa's shoulders stiffened, and he immediately regretted putting her in defensive mode. "I get enough."

Her tone shut the conversation down. He let it go for now, but he promised to himself that he would find a way for Tessa to have some time for herself to enjoy life. He hadn't been able to do that for his own dad growing up, but maybe he could do something for her.

Luke was deep in thought, and he didn't notice Tessa reaching out with a finger to swipe paint on his nose until it was too late.

"No, you didn't just do that."

Tessa giggled. "I did. You were looking too serious and grumpy over there. Stop worrying about me. I chose this life. I'm happy."

She may be happy, but she could be happier. Luke would think on it, but for now, he had some revenge to take. He dipped his finger in the paint and waggled it at her.

Tessa's eyes widened. "Don't you dare."

"You started it," he said as he stalked closer to her.

"I'm sorry, okay? You don't need to get me back. I'll get you something to wash the paint off with."

He leaned forward and painted the tip of her nose, then a smiley face on her cheek. "Get enough for two."

Tessa scowled at him for a minute, and Luke briefly wondered if he had gone too far in his revenge. But it seemed she couldn't hold in her glower for long. "I suppose I deserved that one."

Her laugh filled the room, and he joined her.

"I really should clean this up. Because if the kids see this, they will think a paint fight is perfectly acceptable," she said.

Luke shuddered at the thought of a roomful of kids with free reign over paint buckets. "Yeah we wouldn't want that."

Tessa went to clean it off first, and when it was finally Luke's turn, he stared at himself wide eyed in the mirror. He not only had paint on his face, but his hair was disheveled beyond all recognition. While he prided himself in being put together most of the time, just a few days with Tessa, Tommy and all the amazing kids in this home had gotten him to loosen up a bit.

He just wasn't sure if he liked it or not. Heading back to the toddlers' room, he stopped when he heard Tessa singing along with the radio while painting. A surge of happiness filled his heart, and it hit him that this place might really be good for him after all.

Chapter Six

Forty-seven. Tessa had yawned forty-seven times in the past three hours, Luke noted on Saturday. He knew this because he had been counting. Her quick dismissal of his concerns about lack of time to rest only increased his awareness of how much Tessa took on. It had to be hard taking care of all these kids and the house, and paying the bills.

How is she paying the bills? That question had gnawed at him throughout the rest of the day. Unfortunately, it slipped from his mouth during lunch. Tessa didn't seem to think it was rude at all, however.

"Oh, I get a subsidy from the state to run the group home," Tessa said. "It isn't much, but it helps."

A four-year-old named Emma handed him the bowl of vegetables after she took only one to put it on her plate. "Mama T also works very hard at night helpin' people. That's how she gets to buy us all the snacks and stuff."

Luke arched an eyebrow at that. "Oh? What does she do to help people?"

Tessa's face turned bright red. "It's nothing."

Zack shook his head. "No, Mama T, it's good! You tell people how things will help them out! You're always on the phone. I hear you from my room."

Tessa sighed. "You're supposed to be asleep when that happens."

The little boy grinned. "I always stay awake for a while."

Luke didn't want the subject to get too far off course. "So you have a night job too?"

He couldn't imagine her having the energy to also work with all she maintained in her life.

Tessa wouldn't meet his eyes, but she nodded. "It's not a big deal. I do a telemarketing job after the kids are in bed."

If she worked a night job and got up early for the kids… when did she actually sleep? The math wasn't adding up. "What time do you get up in the morning?"

She cringed. "The kids and I get up about six thirty to get them ready for school and out the door."

Zack spoke up again. "But Mama T gets up earlier and cleans up the house. I hear her every day."

Luke's frown turned into a scowl. "So how late do you work at night?"

He was starting to see a bigger picture as to why this woman looked so exhausted and disheveled all the time.

"Oh, I usually work from like seven until 1:00 a.m. or so," Tessa said.

Shock rolled through his system. "You only get about four or five hours of sleep at night?"

That definitely did not seem like enough. No wonder she had circles under her eyes and couldn't stop yawning.

Her chin lifted stubbornly. "I get by. I have to earn some extra money."

"Extra money for what? Doesn't the state pay you for all these kids?"

Zack's eyes bulged at his question, and Emma's lip quivered. Other eyes darted toward Tessa questioningly.

Luke apologized immediately. This conversation was something that shouldn't be held in front of little ears.

"Let's put a pin in this and talk about it later," he said, and her shoulders dropped immediately in relief.

Luke knew she was probably hoping they could change to a different subject. But he couldn't let it go. It didn't seem right that she was working herself to the bone. He had to do something to help her.

Once they cleared the table and got the younger kids down for a nap, they settled the older ones down with a movie. Luke cornered Tessa as she tiptoed out of one of the toddler's rooms. They were all so excited about the new paint colors and the fact that they were bunking together during the project that it was hard to get them settled for naptime.

"Okay, back to our earlier conversation—when exactly is it that you sleep, Tessa?"

She frowned at him, clearly annoyed that the conversation had returned to this.

"Well, usually I can take a nap during the time that the little ones are asleep during the day," Tessa said.

He narrowed his eyes. "Why aren't you doing that now?"

She shrugged. "Well, you're here. And also, it's the weekend, so someone has to watch the older kids," Tessa said. "During the school week when they are gone, I can usually catch an hour or so during toddler and baby naptime."

Luke folded his arms over his chest. "But I'm here, so I can watch them. And you can," he said, steering toward the only room he hadn't gone in yet, which he assumed was her bedroom, "go take a nap. I don't want to see you again until those dark circles under your eyes are gone."

She shook her head. "That wouldn't be fair of me to put all that responsibility on you."

Irritation churned in Luke's belly. "But you take on that responsibility all the time, so much responsibility. Too much, if you ask me. I'm watching the kids. You go take a nap."

Finally, she gave in and headed toward her room. Something nagged at him that he had to know before she went to sleep.

"Tessa, why do you have to work so many hours? Do they really not pay to take care of these kids?"

She grimaced. "Yeah, they do, but the money usually comes well after a placement. Sometimes they are not even here anymore when they process it. I need stuff to make them comfortable when they first get here."

She wiped a hand over her exhausted face before continuing, "These kids come into care with nothing but the clothes on their backs. And, in the case of a lot of fosters, they have a trash bag that they take their stuff from home to home in. It's not right. It's not fair."

Tessa looked angry right now, her face flushed and her hands on her hips. Luke could feel his anger at the way the system tossed around these kids start to rise too.

"I want every kid that comes into my care to have clothes that belong to them. Not clothes that have to stay here when they move on to somewhere else. I want them to have a suitcase of their own," Tessa explained. "If they move back home, it's theirs to keep. If they move to another foster home, they have something to carry their things. Something that belongs to them. It's so important to me, and that's why I work the extra hours."

Luke had no idea what to say in response to her speech.

He couldn't believe the sacrifices this woman made for the kids in her care. She was a good woman, and he wanted to do something to help. "Maybe I can donate some of my overtime to help the cause too. Or start a fundraising campaign."

She stiffened her shoulders, and he held up his hand before she could object. "I know, I know—you don't like to ask for help. But it seems like this project is getting a little bit bigger than one person can shoulder. Besides, you've had me involved for several days now. And I think it's working out well."

She gave him a smile. "Yeah, you've been a big help this week. And I gotta say, having the other volunteers around the house from your church has been really amazing."

She paused for a moment, her brows furrowed. "So I guess if you want to start something, I suppose I'll be okay with it."

Luke felt his heart lighten. Not only was she becoming accustomed to having helpers in the house, but she also wasn't fighting support off anymore. He liked to think he was having a positive impact on her. Well, he would if she didn't look like she was going to collapse at any moment now.

"There, agreeing with me wasn't so hard, was it?" he teased. "Now, let's keep that trend going, and you head on in there and sleep."

Tessa rolled her eyes but didn't disagree with him. She went into the room and didn't come out until several hours later, looking refreshed.

"I can't believe I slept that long! Were they good for you?"

Luke nodded. "They were fine. We just watched a movie. You obviously slept long because you needed it."

She arched a brow. "Is this your way of saying 'I told you so?'"

He covered a laugh with a cough. "Um…you said it, not me."

Tessa elbowed him and laughed. "Okay, okay, you were right. I admit it. I did need some rest. You want to help me get the kids a snack?"

Once everyone was fed and went outside for some fun, Luke helped Tessa clean up in the kitchen. He probably should go home soon. But he couldn't leave a mess behind. It went completely against his nature. Besides, he was having a good day. The thought of going home to his quiet and empty house wasn't appealing to him at all.

A loud scream from outside tore him from his thoughts. Luke and Tessa locked their eyes on each other before taking off toward the yard in a sprint.

Tessa's heart raced as she ran toward the backyard. Something terrible was happening, if the follow-up screams coming from the children were any indication. Luke was a few paces in front of her, and he halted once he entered the yard.

Tessa ran smack into his back. She was going to push him out of the way to help whoever was in trouble when a booming laugh came out of him.

"Nothing to worry about," he said.

She didn't believe him. "What?"

She peeked around him and was rewarded with a face full of water. Luke laughed even harder.

"The kids are just having a good old-fashioned water fight," he said.

Tessa sputtered as the water dripped down her face. She

hadn't been planning on this for activity time, but it was an unseasonably warm day, so why not?

Zack had the hose and was spraying the other kids with it. They were shrieking from both fear and delight every time the cold water hit them. Luke had walked backward onto the porch. Tessa bit back a smile. *Doesn't want to mess up his perfect-looking outfit.*

She nudged him. "You were telling me I needed more time for fun and relaxation. What about you? Can you let loose and have fun too?"

He grinned while rolling up his sleeves. "Oh, you have no idea what you just started."

Zack let out a yelp as Luke pulled the hose right out of his hands and went straight into attack mode. He sprayed Tessa in the face first, and she dropped her jaw in shock.

"You couldn't give me five minutes to recover from my last dousing?"

Luke gave her a mischievous grin. "All's fair in war. Tessa…kids… I only have one thing to say to you."

They all waited in anticipation until he leaned forward and, with a menacing growl to his voice, said, "Run."

Tessa giggled as the kids squealed and took off in different directions. Luke proceeded to get every child in the yard completely soaked. With perfect aim.

"He's good! Everyone take cover!" Zack yelled.

They all dodged behind various toys in the yard. When Luke turned on her, Tessa realized she was a sitting duck. She needed to find somewhere to go. When one of the kids distracted him, she scurried to the side of the house and hid behind a bush. Unfortunately, many of the leaves had already fallen off for the fall, and he spotted her right away. He sprayed her again.

Once she stopped sputtering, she gave him a fake glower, trying to look very serious and upset and not at all thinking this was the most fun she had had in a long time. "How are you so good at this? You're so regimented and organized all the time. I would have thought a water fight was totally out of your wheelhouse."

His booming laugh sounded again at that. It made her serious demeanor break.

"What's so funny?" she asked.

"You decided to pick a water fight with someone who uses a fire hose for a living," Luke said.

She groaned. Why hadn't she thought of that?

"Do you give up?" he asked.

Tessa put her hands up in surrender. "I think we are no match for your skills."

Everyone else in the yard gave up, especially when the sun was starting to set and the air started to cool. "You guys go inside and change. I'll put the hose away," Tessa said.

But just as she was grabbing it from Luke, Zack twisted the handle, accidentally turning the water up rather than down. A big spray hit both of them in the face. Tessa was screaming and laughing at the same time. She hadn't known such a sound was possible.

"Turn it the other way, pal!" Luke shouted in between laughs.

Tessa couldn't remember the last time she and the kids had so much fun. Luke was definitely a great addition to the house. She had thought he was such an orderly and organized person when they first met. But seeing him loosen up a little was great.

It would be a little lonely the next few days without him while he was on shift at the station. Another scream pulled

Tessa from her thoughts. She wasn't in a panic this time, however, because of the recent false alarm.

But when she turned toward the house, she saw little Emma on the ground, clutching her knee. Tessa rushed over to her.

"What happened, honey?" she asked, crouching in front of the girl.

Emma took several shuddering, sobbing breaths before she could get the words out. Tessa wiped her tears, waiting patiently for the little one to speak.

"My toe got stuck on the step and I fell, and now I'm bleeding," she said, the last two words said on a wail.

Tessa grimaced when she saw the loose bit of brick near the steps. Just another thing to get fixed around here. "Let me see it," she said, pulling Emma's hand away. Sure enough, it was a classic skinned knee. Nothing that warranted a trip to the emergency department, but it still needed to be bandaged up.

"Professional firefighter here and certified boo-boo mender," Luke said. "I've got a first aid kit in my truck."

Tessa snorted at that. "You think I have this many kids and don't have a first aid kid in every room of the house?"

She kissed Emma's knee and wiped tears from her face. "Do you want Luke to fix you up?"

Emma nodded, wiping at her eyes. "But can he use the mermaid bandage?"

Tessa smiled. "I'm sure those are his favorite."

She turned to Luke. "In the upstairs bathroom, under the sink. If you could grab that kit and patch her up, I would appreciate it. That will give me a chance to start the paperwork on this."

His eyebrows shot up. "Paperwork? Over a skinned knee?"

Tessa nodded. "Yeah, we have to fill out a form with every single injury each kid gets…no matter how big or small. Even the tiniest of cuts. We have to keep records of it all. I have to document everything while they are in my care. It's a foster parent rule," she explained.

Luke frowned. "I can't believe they make you do all that work. It's not like you don't have a million other things to do."

She shrugged. "Well, we have to prove that the kids are safe with us. And this is one thing I don't want to mess up."

Especially with the big inspection coming up, Tessa thought.

"She tripped on this loose stair. I'm worried about this and all the other repairs I have to make around here. They're just going to label this place as a safety hazard."

Luke's face was stern as he scooped the pouting Emma up in his arms. "That's totally wrong, though, and a whole bunch of people will come to your defense if that happens. You do everything in your power to take care of these kids and make sure they have a happy and safe home."

But Tessa couldn't quell the nerves that roiled within her as she watched Luke carry the crying little girl away. Sure, she did give her all in making this a good home for the children. But she couldn't help wondering if it was enough. If she herself was enough.

Chapter Seven

"Do you think if I raised enough money, you could cut down your shift by an hour or two every day?" Luke asked.

Tessa rubbed her temples. The firefighter had stayed through dinner and helped with bedtime. Now, as she was preparing to log into work, his questions about her schedule returned.

"Maybe. I don't know. But please don't do that. Between all the cleaning and repairs everyone is doing here…if you ask for money, I'm just going to come across as needy," she explained.

As someone who had grown up in the foster system, Tessa hated for people to think that she was needy or desperate. She had been told so many times in her life that she should be grateful for every little thing and that she didn't deserve the kindness strangers were giving her.

"It's not needy. You have a great ministry here, and people will want to help out," Luke protested.

She knew that this subject was like a broken record with him. As long as he continued to come here to visit her youngest charge, he would be trying to pressure her into accepting more help. Part of her wanted it to end so she could go back to her overworked and non-scrutinized life.

"It's fine, Luke. I like the work. It lets me be a normal adult for part of the day," she said with a forced chuckle. Maybe if she made light of the situation, he would leave it alone.

The truth was, she was exhausted. Tessa didn't know how long she could sustain working this job and caring for the kids. Her reserves of energy were running out. She would need to cut her hours soon, especially if she kept getting emergency newborn placements in the middle of the night. She needed to be available to welcome kids into her home at any and all hours.

Something would work out. It just had to. She hadn't worked so long and hard on this group-home project for it to fail now.

Even Luke being here this week and the other volunteers had shown her that she didn't have to do this all alone. But accepting help and accepting money were two different things.

"Um, I don't mean to be rude…but I have to log onto the phones," Tessa said.

Luke's shoulders fell in resignation. She wondered why this all bothered him so much. "Okay, I'll get out of your hair. But please promise to try to get some sleep."

She gave him a mock salute. "Yes, Captain."

He rolled his eyes. "Well, Private, you can't be on duty twenty-four seven. Every good soldier needs some R & R."

Luke gave her a wave. As he headed out the door, he reminded her that he wouldn't be around for a few days. He had a shift at the fire station, which usually meant a couple of overnights.

Tessa promised him she would survive just fine without him, but he still looked worried.

"I've been doing this for a long time without your help," she said grumpily.

He just smiled and winked. "Yeah, but now that I'm involved, you're not going to get rid of me that easily."

After he was gone, she logged into the phone queue. A lot of these late-night calls were customer complaints that she was supposed to try to upsell more services to for the IT company she worked for. And she answered the chat system as well. She was surprised how many customers stayed up exceedingly late when they had computer problems. Tessa would give anything to be in a bed right now.

"Hello? Are you even listening to me?" an angry voice said on the other side of the line. She'd just closed her eyes for a second and must have dozed off. Maybe Luke was right. Maybe she was wearing herself too thin. But she had no idea what to do about it.

Just get through the state inspection. And then you can figure out how to handle this. One problem at a time.

That thought was easier said than done, as problems seemed to pile up exponentially. Tessa had a feeling that after the visit next month, everything would be different. Whether that difference was for the good or for the bad, she didn't know.

On Sunday, Luke went to church before heading into his shift at the fire station. So many people came up to him and offered to help at Harmony House. He imagined it would be difficult for Tessa to find something for all of them to do, if she let down her guard enough to accept even more assistance.

Even the pastor asked after the group home when Luke greeted him on the way out of the church.

"Some of the kids have come to Vacation Bible School from time to time, but we haven't been able to connect with their foster mother to help much until now," Pastor Hartman said. "Thank you for providing an open door for us to reach out to her."

Luke nodded. "Tessa is a kind and generous woman… but she's working herself so hard for those kids. I hope we can continue to lend a helping hand after the state inspection is over."

The pastor clapped Luke on the shoulder. "That's a great idea. Some of our members have been talking about starting a foster parent–support team. I think your friend Tessa and her group home might just be what we need to get the program started."

He was thankful that even after Tommy and his reason for daily visits to Harmony House was over, Luke would still have a lasting impact on the place.

"I think it would mean a lot. I've been going over there often, and the kids could use more adults in their lives to care for them," Luke said.

He frowned, wondering if that made it sound like Tessa wasn't doing a good job. "I mean, their foster mother is very loving and caring—"

Pastor Hartman held up his hand. "You don't need to defend her to me, son. People in this congregation have been singing her praises and talking about that group home of hers all week. It's a good thing she's got going there. And we need more people like her in the world. But you're right—the more people who can be there to support these kids, the better."

Luke gave the pastor a smile. "Well, they have a foster

mother…but they could probably use all the foster grand-parents they can get."

The older man laughed. "They will be the most spoiled kids in the county."

Luke thought of Zack, Tommy, Emma and the others surrounded by older people who doted on them. The image warmed his heart. They deserved that. What they did not deserve were the circumstances that had landed them in foster care.

"Did you hear about the baby who was left at the fire station?"

The pastor nodded. "Yeah, your dad told me about how you named little Tommy after him. He's been bragging about it all over town."

Luke chuckled. "If I had known that he'd get a big head about it, I might have changed my mind. Little Tommy… He's special. I don't see how his mom could just give him up like that."

The last parishioners, who must have sensed that this serious conversation canceled out any goodbyes they were going to get from the pastor, left the auditorium. Pastor Hartman gestured toward the church's fellowship hall.

"Am I keeping you from something? I have to head to work soon anyway," Luke said.

The double doors opened to reveal a flurry of activity. People ran by with boxes of canned goods and bags of clothes.

"You're not keeping me at all, but we need to continue this conversation while I sort cans. It's our Blessings Sunday today, and it is just about to start."

Luke couldn't believe that he had forgotten. He had a bag of donations at home. On the first Sunday of every month, the church opened up its doors and did a food bank and clothing giveaway for those in need in the community. Across the fellowship hall, he could see his father setting up a chair and his razor set. He couldn't do fancy haircuts, but he offered free army-style buzz cuts to anyone who wanted them. The same look Luke had grown up with during his childhood.

He ran his hand through his hair, grateful he didn't need to keep it so close to his scalp anymore. Maybe his childhood in a military man's house was not 100 percent perfect after all. *But it was pretty close*, he thought.

The pastor cleared his throat, drawing Luke's attention back to their conversation. "So, back to the baby you mentioned. We don't know the circumstances that led to him being left there. But I think that God brought that young man into your life for a reason."

Luke snorted. "Yeah, I was the one who was on watch duty that night."

The older man shook his head. "And this baby just happened to be dropped on the night you would welcome him. From what your father is saying, you've taken quite a shine to the boy."

It was hard for Luke to put into words the connection he felt with little Tommy. "I've gotten attached to him pretty quickly. And I think he likes me too. I'm the only one who can get him to stop crying…well, besides his foster mom, Tessa."

The pastor chuckled. "Well, that's saying something. I can't wait to see how God continues to use you in little Tommy's life. I have a feeling it goes just beyond his baby years."

Luke's brow furrowed. "No, he's going to go to a permanent family soon. I don't think they will want a random firefighter hanging out with him all the time."

The very thought of not seeing the little guy anymore made Luke's heart ache, as if he was feeling the grief of that moment already. But what right did he have to grieve over a baby he just met? Who had a whole future without him?

"You never know. I think God has a plan for the two of you. It's going to be something to watch," the pastor said with a wink.

Luke dismissed his words. His pastor may be wise, but he didn't know everything about the situation. "I have a plan for my life, and this baby isn't part of it. I'll be there when he needs me, but he has his own family waiting for him out there somewhere."

The older man studied him carefully. "You have your own plans? What if they aren't the same as God's?"

What was he getting at? Panic started to stir in Luke's stomach as he considered the question.

"I have been waiting patiently for God to give me the life I've been praying for," Luke said.

The pastor laid a hand on Luke's shoulder. "You seem a little angry, son."

Maybe I am, a little bit, Luke thought. "It's just… I want to have kids of my own someday. Being around Tommy and the kids this week has been great. But it just reminded me of what I'm missing in my life. And someone had my dream—they had a beautiful baby, and they just threw him away like he was trash."

A nearby gasp drew Luke's attention to the end of the table, where a teenage girl was standing with a couple of food cans in her hands. She was covered in dirt, her disheveled hair pulled up into a ponytail on top of her head. The teen also had several of the cookies from the snack table stuffed into her mouth. *Poor thing, she must be starving.* Luke wondered if she was living on the streets right now or if her home situation was rough.

"Is there anything we can get you? Do you need more food…clothes?" he asked.

The girl just stared at him wide eyed and shook her head. Tears started rolling down her cheeks. His firefighter instincts told him this young woman was in pain…but he couldn't help her unless she let them know what the problem was. He tried again.

Luke filled a box with food and slowly handed it to the girl, hoping to not spook her.

"Do you need to talk to someone? If neither of us will do, there are some ladies—"

"Not trash," the girl's scratchy voice interrupted.

"Excuse me?"

Both he and the pastor leaned forward to hear more. "We didn't catch that, sweetheart. What about the trash?"

The girl squeezed the box tightly into her chest and let out a breath. "He's not trash, and I didn't have a choice."

Luke froze. Was she talking about… Tommy? Before he could open his mouth to ask a follow-up question, the girl turned and ran from the building, muffled sobs in her wake.

"Was that… Tommy's mom?"

Pastor Hartman was already walking swiftly after the girl. Luke could have kicked himself. He should have followed her too. She was moving so quickly that he was sure the pastor wouldn't catch up with her in time.

His guess proved correct when the older man returned a moment later, out of breath. "She got away from me. She's really scared."

Luke felt a little guilty for his harsh words. He didn't know what that young woman had to do with little Tommy, but something he had said about the safe baby drop had set her off.

"Do you know that girl?" he asked. He needed to call Sierra at CPS and let her know what had happened. Maybe they could track the young woman down.

Pastor Hartman shook his head. "This was her first time at the food bank. I've never seen her before."

Luke stared at the doors of the fellowship hall, hoping the girl would change her mind and return. He suddenly had the urge to go over to Tessa's and snuggle Tommy close. But he had to go to work.

The only thing that made him feel slightly better was that he knew the young boy would still be getting plenty of love from one of the kindest women he had ever met. Tommy was safe and adored in Tessa's home. No matter where he came from, God had at least blessed the little baby with the right person to care for him.

Chapter Eight

On his way to work, Luke called Sierra and told him about the incident with the young woman at church. "I think that she may be related to the baby or know who is," he explained.

Sierra was quiet for a moment. "Or she could be his mother."

If that was true, then Luke had truly messed up in saying what he had about Tommy's mother throwing him away like trash. The pastor was right—he didn't know what the baby's mother was going through or why she'd felt desperate enough to leave her child behind.

The young lady he had seen at church, she had to still be a teenager, or barely an adult. If she was indeed Tommy's mother—or sister or whatever—she needed support, not anger.

"I hope I didn't scare her away," he said.

Sierra was quick to reassure him. "Safe-haven babies come with a lot of emotions. And not just from post-birth hormones. Tommy's mother—whether it's this girl or someone else—is probably feeling a mix of fear, sadness, anxiety, grief, loss and more."

Luke thought of little Tommy, knowing that anyone giving up the opportunity to be in that boy's life would indeed be opening the door to grief. "I understand. He's going to be hard to walk away from some day."

She made a humming sound on the other end of the phone. "Are you planning on leaving Tommy's life?"

This wasn't the first time this week he had to think about that question. And the more he considered never seeing Tommy again, the less likely it became.

"Maybe whoever adopts him will let me stay in his life," Luke said. He had said something similar to Tessa, but now his tone sounded a little more desperate.

"I'm sure they will. You are a good man, and who wouldn't want such a good influence around their son?" Sierra said.

Son.

The word resonated with Luke and sank to the bottom of his gut.

Someone would be calling Tommy their son. And for some reason, that didn't feel right to him.

Because… Tommy felt like he belonged to Luke already. Like he was his son.

And suddenly, as soon as that thought crossed his mind, Luke wondered if that was at all possible. He wasn't ready to be a father; none of this was in his life plan. But it didn't hurt to ask. "Sierra…what would I…hypothetically…have to do if I wanted to adopt Tommy?"

Once the words were out of his mouth, he wished he could take them back because it felt like there was no return. And he had never gone off his life plan before. Not once.

"Well, you would have to get a home inspection, and since he's a foster kiddo, you would have to go to the mandatory parent training," Sierra explained. "And even then…"

Her hesitancy at the end made him nervous. "And even then, what?"

Sierra cleared her throat. "Most people want to adopt babies. We have a lot of kids in the foster care system who are not babies and who get skipped over by waiting families once someone comes along who's under a year old and available for adoption."

She made it sound like babies were hot commodities rather than actual people. "That's kind of…messed up."

Sierra agreed. "It's so hard to see great kids skipped over because families just want babies. It breaks my heart every time."

Luke thought of Zack. That kid was amazing and deserved the best of families. And he thought of Tommy, being fought over like a prized possession. "So that means once you put up Tommy for adoption…"

"There will be plenty of families that will want to be on the list," Sierra finished.

Which meant he probably didn't stand a chance…not that he was interested in adopting, anyway. *This is all just hypothetical*, he told himself.

"And me being a single man…"

He knew the answer before she said it.

"The state would probably choose a married couple over you," Sierra admitted. "I don't love it, but…it's the system I have to work with."

Luke's shoulders sank. He hadn't really been keen on swerving away from his life plan, but hearing that it was not really a possibility also stung. Still, he knew that there was some sort of connection between Tommy and him. He just didn't know what that would look like in the future.

He would have to pray about it.

No, he would have to pray for that little guy to have the best life ever.

"I understand. Thanks for explaining it to me," Luke said, his voice not betraying the melancholy that filled him.

"I'm really sorry, but if you're interested in doing foster care in the future, I think you would be great at it."

Luke shook his head even though Sierra couldn't see him. That definitely wasn't in his plans. He could not live in the chaos that Tessa did every day.

"Um…let's not get too ahead of ourselves," he said.

Sierra laughed. "You know I've always got to try. We've got a shortage of good foster homes right now. That's why what Tessa's doing is so important. Last year, we had kids going to a shelter, and had some sleeping on cots in our office."

Normally, he would have found it hard to believe that there were so many families in crisis that would need that kind of intervention, but he saw so much trauma daily with his job.

"I will pray that not only Tommy but all those kids find the best possible home for them. Whether through family reunification or with an adoption."

He got off the phone with Sierra after promising to let her know if he saw the young woman from church again. He arrived at work just in time, running into his friend Sam, who was coming out of the locker room.

"There he is! Haven't seen you in a few days since you left with that baby in your arms," Sam said. "We were beginning to think something happened to you."

Luke shook his head. "No, I had some time off this week, and I've been volunteering over at the group home where little Tommy went."

Sam arched a brow at that. "Tommy? Why do I feel like I've missed a lot?"

His friend agreed to go to the station's kitchen and pour them some coffee while Luke changed into his uniform. Once they both were sitting down, Luke explained everything that had happened during the past several days.

Sam's eyes widened as he told the story. "This is all so… spontaneous and not at all like you."

Luke couldn't help but laugh. "You're right…and I don't hate it. But I definitely couldn't live in a house like that. I like things in their place. I like the quiet."

Sam chuckled. "Maybe this is God's way of shaking up your life. Maybe He's trying to get you used to this because it's in your future."

"Absolutely not. I still know the exact kind of woman I want to marry and the way I want our future to look," Luke said firmly. He crossed his arms, as if warding off any other possibilities.

"What about this foster mother who featured a lot in your story? Does she fit into this ideal of yours?" Sam asked.

Luke sighed. "Tessa? No, she's the complete opposite of my dream girl. She's wild and unorganized and spontaneous."

And pretty. And kind. And a wonderful mother. Luke shook his head to knock these extra descriptors for Tessa aside.

Sam studied him carefully. "I think maybe it's time for you to change your expectations for a wife. Maybe you need to stop thinking about who you think is your perfect woman and be open to someone that God might put in your path."

Luke frowned. "I doubt God would put someone like Tessa in my life."

Sam laughed. "It kind of sounds like He already did."

He and Tessa were just friends. There was no way they could ever be anything more—their way of doing things was just too different. Sam simply didn't understand how important his life plan was. It was what had informed most of his choices. Becoming a fireman...stable job: check. Nice, organized house: check. He had two of the life goals done already. If he veered off his perfect plan, which had gotten him where he was now...it could lead to chaos.

Luke shook his head at how close he had come to doing just that earlier today, when he'd asked about adopting Tommy. Sierra telling him that it was unlikely... Maybe that was God's way of telling him to stay the course.

Sam clapped him on the back. "You're thinking about this way too hard. All I'm saying is that you should be open to possibilities. No need to panic over the idea."

"I'm not panicking. Well, maybe a little because I saw Sawyer was on kitchen duty today. Remember how gross it was last time?"

Thankfully, Sam took the hint in his change of subject. "Yeah, well, maybe we can convince him to get takeout."

His stomach growling, Luke followed his friend to the door. "Now that's a plan I think we can both get on board with."

Two days later, Tessa was woken up from her nap by the sound of knocking on her door. Her brow furrowed as she rushed down the stairs. She wasn't expecting anyone at this hour. When she pulled open the door, she was surprised to see a man in a suit standing there. Based on the stern expression on his wrinkled face, she didn't think this was going to be a pleasant visit.

"Miss Duncan, I am Ted Stanton, one of the home inspectors for the state," he said, his voice monotone, like he would rather be anywhere else than here.

Tessa's stomach clenched in panic. State inspection? They weren't supposed to be here for a few weeks. Her home was nowhere near ready for an inspection.

"Oh… I wasn't expecting you," she said. Mentally, she made a note of every single mess that the kids had made in the house that morning. She knew that lived-in clutter didn't disqualify a foster home, but she still wanted it to look nearly perfect every time they came.

"Yes, that's generally how it works. We try to surprise people so they don't hide things from us. That's why I found it highly odd that you were given such a lengthy warning about the one later this month," Mr. Stanton said.

Great, Sierra's heads-up must have triggered some warning bells somewhere, Tessa thought.

"Well, come on in, I guess," Tessa said, gesturing him inside. "The babies are still asleep, so please keep your voice low."

Not that the man showed any sign of being loud enough to wake anyone. He pulled a clipboard from his bag. Tessa walked around, picking up various toys off the floor. "Sorry it's a bit messy."

The man finally showed a little warmth in his eyes. "I'm actually not here for an official inspection, so there is really no need to be anxious. Your case worker asked me to come and do a trial inspection. I'm going to make a list of everything that needs to be done."

His steady gaze darted to different points in the room. "And hopefully, you can get them fixed in the next few weeks."

Tessa's heart rate started to return to its regular rhythm. She was a little annoyed at Sierra for not telling her that this was happening, but Mr. Stanton was right—they seldom had much warning. The fact that she got notice of the one later this month was a miracle in and of itself.

This man, though he looked grumpy, was still a blessing because he would tell her just what to focus on. Sierra knew exactly what she needed. She thanked God for sending her not only an amazing case worker but also a friend.

It was hard to try not to peek at Mr. Stanton's list as he stood in her living room and started writing what looked to be a novel.

Calm down, she told herself. *You're just overthinking things. Really, there shouldn't be too much to do. Maybe that's what he's going to tell you.*

"I can see your front steps have a few bricks coming loose," Mr. Stanton said. "I wasn't even in the house yet and made note of several things that need to be done."

Tessa bit her lip to fight the sob that threatened to escape. She had not been overthinking things at all. Maybe she had been underthinking. Still, she tried to remain calm as she followed the man throughout the house. She did fidget every time he wrote something down on his pad or made a "Hmm…" noise.

He did follow her instructions to remain quiet near the kids' rooms. His normally stern face softened when he caught sight of them sleeping safely in their cribs.

It dropped back into a scowl in the hallway when he ripped five pages out of his notebook and handed them to her. "You have a lovely home, Ms. Duncan. I can see all the love and care you put into taking care of the children and this place."

She knew there was a *but* coming.

"However…" he said.

Close enough, she thought of her prediction.

"This house is also an old one. And there are things that need to be fixed if it is going to continue to meet the needs and be a safe place for children in the years to come. The state wants this home to be an example, so there are a few things you're going to need to do to bring it up to par."

Tessa looked down at the five pages in her hand. There were definitely more than "a few things" on the list. She thanked Mr. Stanton and saw him to the door. Once the man was gone, she sank down to the floor, leaning her head against the wall.

"What am I going to do?"

She thought of her new friend Luke and what he would do in this situation, and she decided to give it a try. "God, I know that I don't pray to You often, but please, please help me get all this done so my kids have their home."

Despite being inexperienced at prayer, a peace filled Tessa. It would be okay. She somehow knew it would. She pulled out her phone and sent a quick text to Luke.

I think our list of things to fix around here just got a lot longer. Bring your screwdriver over when you're rested up after shift if you still want to help.

He didn't respond right away, so she just assumed he

was busy. Tessa busied herself getting Tommy up and giving him a bottle.

She tried to enjoy his happy gurgles as he played with her hair while drinking, but her eyes kept drifting to that list. Tessa knew that it would all get done, but where to start?

There was a knock at the door, and she hurried to open it, worried that it was the inspector coming back to tell her all the things she had done wrong.

But to her surprise, Luke was standing there with a big toolbox in his arms and a grin on his face. Behind him were six firemen, all with their own sets of tools.

"Wh-what…?" she said with a stutter. "What are you doing here?"

Luke just gave her a wink and turned to the other men. "Let's get started."

He stepped aside to let the entire crew into the house, leaving Tessa standing at the door with her mouth open.

Chapter Nine

"I'll just take that," Luke said as he pulled the list out of Tessa's hand. She gasped, finally pulled out of her shock at the group of firemen now standing in the living room.

"Have you got any pushpins?"

It took her a moment to process what he was talking about, but she finally pointed to the display board in the kitchen where she posted the kids' schedules. Luke was still looking over the list and nodding while one of the other firefighters grabbed the pins.

Luke took them and pinned the five pages on the wall.

"What are you doing? Why are you here so soon? I thought you were on shift?" Tessa asked.

Luke shrugged. "We called in some favors and got the next crew to come in a little early once I got your text."

She pointed to the big metal green box in his hands. "So you rushed over with your toolboxes? It wasn't even that big of an emergency."

He laughed. "You actually asking for help means something. I figured you might be a bit overwhelmed."

"And you brought the whole crew?"

Luke nodded. "You know you have a night job to help

pay the bills? Well, sometimes we firemen have to do that too. We have a whole firefighter-handyman service."

She looked back and forth between each one of the men, who were watching her conversation with Luke with interest. "Thank you so much for hurrying over here when you must be exhausted from work, but I can't afford to pay you."

Luke scowled at her. "You don't need to pay us. We're all here to help. We want to."

The men around him all nodded, some put down their toolboxes and folded their arms stubbornly. *It's like a whole group of Lukes*, she thought. *I can't possibly argue with them all.*

He must have sensed her surrender, because he turned to his crew and started handing out marching orders. "All right, gents. You see all the lists. We need to get started."

Luke told them they were going to work on the house from top to bottom, starting with the upstairs and working their way down. They all murmured in agreement, and Tessa just stared at them with wide eyes as they tramped up her stairs.

As she went to close the door, Luke called to her over his shoulder, "I wouldn't do that if I were you. There's another group coming behind us."

"What? I don't understand."

He gave her that infuriating wink again. "Just you wait."

As soon as he went upstairs, another group of people, an eclectic mix of young and older adults, appeared on her doorstep with cleaning supplies in her hands.

"Hello there, dear. So good to see you again. We're here to get started now that we have a more detailed list," said Joan, a woman she had met the other day when the church people had first arrived to help.

"But you guys already did so much to help me. You don't need to spend all your free time here again," Tessa protested.

Joan patted her on the hand. "Now, dear, we love you and the kids, and we want to make this the very best home that we can. Not that it isn't already wonderful. We'll just put some extra polish on it."

Tessa stared at everyone with wide eyes as the people studied the list and started claiming tasks.

"But… I don't understand why you are doing all this for me," she said, so softly that she didn't expect anyone else to hear. She had been alone so often in her life. Having so many people who seemed to…care…was a bit jarring.

Joan wrapped her arms around Tessa and pulled her in for a warm hug. She smelled faintly of butterscotch, which is what Tessa thought every grandmother must smell like. "Because we love you and the kids. And now that you've opened your home to us, we're not going to let you all go."

Tessa blinked back tears. How could someone she had barely met love her and the kids already? She thought briefly of all the terrible foster homes she had been in, where love definitely wasn't present. Her mission was to provide the very kindness Joan was showing her to the kids who were in her care for such a short time. "This was how I wanted my house to work. To teach the kids that kindness is free and they don't have to earn it."

Joan pulled back and smiled at her, cupping Tessa's cheek. "From what I've seen, dear, you have some learning to do in that department as well. No fear—we've adopted you into our family now. And you're not getting rid of us."

Before she could respond, a cry came from one of the

rooms. Joan frowned. "Oh, no, did we wake them up with all our activity?"

Tessa glanced down at her watch. "No, it's just about time for their nap to be over. They are probably hungry for their snack."

But once she got all the little ones up, the toddlers were too excited about all the visitors to eat. Soon, they were roped into being "helpers," meaning they talked each of the older people's ears off while they worked in all parts of the house.

The clamor of excitement didn't die down when the older kids came home from school. They joined in the fun immediately, demanding assignments from Luke and his crew or the cleaners. Listening to the excited chatter and joyful voices of many generations in her home, Tessa's heart warmed. She knew she should be diving into work as well, but she just wandered around, bringing cups of water to everyone with a dopey smile on her face.

"You okay?" Luke asked after downing his entire drink in less than twenty seconds. He and his crew were replacing all the electrical sockets in her room. It hadn't been on the list, but they insisted it needed to be done anyway.

"Yeah, I'm fine. This is just…"

His brow furrowed. "Too much? I'm sorry, maybe we should have staggered the amount of people who were here at one time."

Tessa reached up and grabbed his hand. It was worn and rough from all the work they had been doing. "No, absolutely not. Just all the people—it's so happy and joyful in here today. It's like a…"

Luke's expression softened. "Community? Family?"

She gave a small smile. "Yeah, that."

"So what's the problem?"

Tessa shook her head, looking down at their still-joined hands. "I've just never really had it much before."

He squeezed her hand gently before letting go. "Well, get used to it, because judging by how excited everyone in my church was to help, I think you're going to be seeing a lot of them."

Tessa thought about the prayer she had said this morning. It seemed as if God had answered already. *Thank You*, she whispered in her head. *This was more than I could have asked for or imagined.*

It turned out that there was one more surprise in store when it came to blessings, because Joan stopped her in the hallway before she went downstairs to refill the waters.

"I hope we haven't come on too strong, Tessa," she said.

"Oh! Not at all! This is really nice." If Tessa had known that this was what would happen if she finally opened up to accepting help, she would have done so a long time ago. An entire community was working together to make this dream of hers come true.

"You know, I have my state fingerprint clearance because I volunteer at my grandkids' school. A lot of the other ladies do too. I know that's a requirement from the state sometimes to be able to watch kids that are in foster care," Joan said.

Tessa nodded. Not all the time, but if it was a regular thing for someone who would be in their lives often, yes, they had to have a background check.

Joan handed her a piece of paper. "We made a list. Our foster care–support group at the church decide that one of the best ways we can help you out long term—if you're okay with it—is if we have someone come by weekly to do some deep cleaning and someone to come watch the kids all day once a week so you can have a day off."

Tessa blinked down at the list of names. "I… I don't need a day off."

The older woman scoffed. "I raised four kids. Every mother needs a day off. You need to get out of this house from time to time. Go soak in some sunshine. Have a cup of coffee without anyone interrupting you with one hundred questions. When was the last time you just sat in silence and relaxed?"

Tessa couldn't remember. It had been a long time. But she didn't know if she could handle the silence. She was used to the constant clamor of the kiddos around her.

But the thought of being able to run errands without having to buckle several car seats was very appealing. And maybe she could go for a walk in the park on one of the new trails by the river… Tessa had been all about her plan for so long, she had no idea what she liked to do for fun. But it might be nice to figure that out.

"That would be lovely, but it's too much," she protested again. "I can't ask all of you to spend so much time here."

"I think that you're stuck with them now," Luke said as he walked down the stairs with a big grin on his face. "Unless you decide to kick them out, they now are a part of this project too."

Once Luke stopped at the foot of the stairs, she surprised herself by wrapping him into a big hug. She wasn't normally one to show this much affection, but the emotions of the day were so overwhelming. "I know I sound like a broken record, but thank you. I don't think I'll be able to say it enough times."

He squeezed her back, and she was lost in the warmth of the hug. "You don't have to say it at all."

Tessa forced her eyes shut to stop the tears that were threatening to spill. Maybe accepting help wasn't so bad after all.

Luke smiled at the scene in the open-concept living and dining rooms and kitchen. Adults and kids were intermingled everywhere, sharing snacks and laughs. Once the little ones finally declared themselves hungry, Tessa made a huge to-do about feeding everyone. A feast of cookies, popcorn and fruit filled the table.

Once everyone had their fill and went back to their tasks, Luke stayed in the kitchen to help her clean up. "I'm sorry this is all a bit much. I probably should have asked."

She snorted. "A heads-up would have been nice, but I'm nothing but grateful. This is great, Luke, truly."

They worked in silence for a while, gathering all the discarded paper plates and cups from around the rooms and tossing them in the trash. "Have you gotten a chance to hold Tommy yet today?"

Luke shook his head. "No, every time I try to find him, he's being swooned over by another grandma."

Tessa giggled. "Well, I think that kiddo will have no shortage of love while he's here."

The immediate reminder that their time in Tommy's life was temporary brought a frown to Luke's face. And a reminder of what had happened at church earlier that week.

"I haven't had time alone to tell you about this...but I think I might have encountered Tommy's family member at church the other day."

Tessa stopped working, her eyes widening. "Really?"

He told her the entire story about the young woman at church. Tessa's chin wobbled a little bit when he mentioned the things he had said about the people who had thrown Tommy away and the girl's reaction. Her compassion for others was written on her face all the time. Luke would never get used to just how kind and good Tessa was.

"Sierra thinks the person we saw might be Tommy's mother," he explained.

Tessa nodded. "It makes sense, based on the way she reacted. Most people who give up their children don't really want to. They feel like they don't have another choice."

Luke waved a hand around the house. "I think we've proven today that there are plenty of people out there willing to help someone in need."

And then an idea sparked in his mind…something that might truly be in Tommy's best interest.

"What if we find her…and help her be able to parent her baby?"

Tessa gave a sad smile. "I think that's a great idea so that she can stay in his life, but we don't want to pressure her to take on more than she can handle."

Luke thought of the sadness in the woman's eyes and the dirt on her clothes. Of the cans in her hands. "Regardless of her kiddo, I think she needs help. She was hungry when we saw her."

What would Tommy think if he found out someday that they had an idea of who his mother was and did nothing to help her?

Tessa laid a hand on his arm. "Well then, we will just have to find her. I will help you look for her."

He arched an eyebrow at that. "You have time for yet another task to add to your workload?"

Tessa grinned at him. "Haven't you heard? I have a baby-sitter squad now."

"Well then, let the search begin, as soon as you have a day off," he said with a chuckle. "Just make sure you save some time for yourself too."

He had a feeling this was a foreign concept for her. Tessa opened her mouth to protest, but her words were cut off by the ringing of his cell phone.

"What's up, Cap?"

The older man on the other line was like a second father to all the men, and Luke knew he wouldn't have interrupted their work here today unless it was important.

"I hate to do this to you all, but there is a major fire at the business complex. We need all hands on deck," Cap said.

"No problem, I'll grab the guys, and we'll be there in a few to grab our gear."

He called the guys down from upstairs and immediately apologized to Tessa. "Sorry to leave you with so much still to do. We will be here whenever we have downtime this week."

Tessa just blinked up at him. "I don't even know what to say. All this…"

"*Thank you* will suffice, though I told you that you don't really have to say it," Luke said. "But maybe you could promise that you will continue to let people help you in the future."

The corners of her lips turned up. "Thank you. And I make no promises."

He scowled. Hadn't she started opening up? "Tessa…"

She laughed at him. "I'm only kidding. Like you said earlier, there's no turning back now."

Luke beamed as young Zack high-fived every fireman

who went out the front door. This place had grown on him too. He eyed Tessa. And the people in it. He had a feeling there was no turning back for him either. His carefully planned out life was getting a wrench thrown into it.

Chapter Ten

Tessa wrote the last thing on her to-do list and smiled down at it. She had a babysitter today and would be able to spend hours outside of the house. She would be able to get so many errands done.

Excitement filled her as she grabbed her keys and her purse. "You sure this is okay?"

"Oh, I'm fine, Tessa. You just go out and have a good time," said Sylvia, one of the ladies who had "adopted" her the other day. Sierra had confirmed that everyone who volunteered to watch the kids had indeed passed their background checks.

"This is going to look great when the inspectors come," the case worker had said when Tessa told her about their rotating babysitting and cleaning schedules. "It shows that the community is embracing programs like this. And most importantly, they are all volunteers, and that doesn't cost the state any money."

Tessa had laughed at that. Money for foster care programs was hard to come by, so having volunteers around was a blessing.

"I don't know how much fun I'll be having at the grocery store, but thank you just the same," Tessa told Sylvia.

The toddlers were all sprawled out on the floor around Sylvia, drawing her a picture of a unicorn-kitty that she'd requested. Some were taking the task very seriously, while others scribbled wildly on the pages. Tessa had no doubt the older woman would declare them all a masterpiece.

"Well, call or text me if you need anything. I'm still going to be in town," Tessa said, having a hard time getting herself to leave. She would need lots of practice to get in the habit of taking more time off.

As she stepped out onto the porch, she ran face-first into a broad chest. She looked up to see Luke standing there. "Oh! I'm so sorry!"

He steadied her and then took a step back. "It's all good, Tess. What are you up to?"

She waved her to-do list. "I'm going to run errands! I have a babysitter."

Luke chuckled. "You are way too excited about that. Let me see that list."

Tessa handed it to him and squawked in protest when he folded it up and tucked it into his back pocket.

"Hey! I need that!"

The infuriating man just shook his head. "No, you don't. Not for a while."

Tessa folded her arms across her chest. "What do you mean?"

Luke sighed. "Tessa, this is your first time off in forever, and you want to use it for errands? No, you have to have fun."

She glared at him. "But I have a list. I thought you loved lists, Mr. Organized."

He chuckled at that, walking toward his truck. Tessa followed him, hoping she could convince him to give her back the list. He reached inside his vehicle and pulled out a piece of paper and a pen. "I do love lists. Which is why I am always prepared to write a new one."

Luke held out the paper and pen to her. "Here."

She took them gingerly and raised an eyebrow. "You want me to...try making a list of new errands? Was mine not well-thought-out enough for you?"

Tessa was so confused right now. Luke laughed and shook his head at her.

"I want you to make a new list. Of all your favorite things to do. If you had no responsibilities in the world and a whole day to yourself...what would you decide to do?"

She sat down on the front step and thought about it. There really wasn't a time in her life when she had nothing to worry about. Even when she was living with her favorite foster mother as a teenager, Tessa had tried to share the load of household responsibilities as much as possible so she wouldn't be a burden.

"Um... I like coffee... I guess," she said.

He sat next to her and nudged her shoulder. "Great. That's an excellent first step. Write it on the list."

She did, then paused on the next line.

"So what's next?"

Tessa thought about it. She would love to restock some of the books on her bedside table. She always took the kids to the library, but she never checked out any for herself because her reading time was sporadic and she could never finish anything before it was due. Still, she loved to read and could use a fresh supply.

Giddiness bubbled inside her. "The bookstore?"

Luke rubbed his hands together. "Now we're talking. What else?"

It took her a few minutes, but Tessa was able to fill out the list with enough things to keep herself busy for a few hours. Still, there was so much other stuff to do.

"All this is great, but someone has to get the groceries—"

Luke guided her toward the passenger side of his car. "I'll tell you what. If we get through at least half of your fun list, I will go with you on all the non-fun errands and help so you get them done faster."

She arched a brow at that. "You're going to spend the day with me?"

He opened the door for her and gestured inside. "Your chariot awaits, milady. Of course I'm going to spend the day with you. Someone needs to make sure you have some fun. I can work on the house later tonight with my buddies."

Tessa didn't have it in her to object, because if she was honest with herself, she probably would return to her errand list if he wasn't there to steer her in the fun direction.

First up, coffee. It was warm and sweet, and she was able to drink it while it was hot, which didn't happen often in her house. She looked up from her cup to see Luke smiling at her.

"What, do I have whipped cream on my nose or something?"

He threw his head back and laughed. "No, I just… I've never seen someone enjoy a cup of coffee quite so much. We definitely have to do this more often."

Tessa felt her cheeks heat. If anyone ran into them now, it might look like they were on a date. "Really?"

"Well, yeah. You don't think I'm going away just because Tommy gets adopted someday, did you?"

She shook her head, wondering what that meant. "Yeah, you've, uh, become such a good friend."

His smile was easy, and she breathed a sigh of relief at not having been too presumptuous. "Yeah, I would say we are good friends now. Besides my whole church and fire-fighter crew, you're stuck with me too."

Tessa didn't think that sounded too bad. "I think I can manage."

He arched a brow. "Are you sure? I can be pretty annoying."

She shook her head. "I haven't seen that yet. Well, other than the time you tried to reorganize my pantry."

Luke laughed. "I promise to avoid reorganizing things until I have your permission."

"Sounds like a plan."

They enjoyed their coffee in silence for a few minutes, and Tessa relished the peace of just being still. With her life, she was constantly on the move. So much to do, with so little time. So many little ones needed her. It felt nice to just relax. Luke was probably right about stealing her other list.

"I did need this," she said, hoping he wouldn't gloat and say *I told you so*.

He surprised her by just nodding. "You did, and I hope you take more days like this in the future."

She just might, especially if she had his company during them. Tessa realized she really didn't know all that much about Luke, other than the bits and pieces he had shared with her in the past week.

"Okay, let's play the random-question game. I ask you something and you have to answer honestly, and you do the same for me."

Luke grinned. "Sounds like fun. You go first."

Tessa thought for a moment. Did she want to start easily…

or hard? "Hmm… What is your favorite memory from child-hood?"

He leaned back in his chair, giving her question some thought. "I have a lot of great ones with me and my dad. But I have to go with one from when my mom was still alive. I don't have a ton of memories of her. But she used to read to me every night before bed. And then she would pray with me and give me one kiss on the forehead for every year old I was. The last one I can remember was when I was four."

His voice choked a little at the end, and Tessa reached out and squeezed his hand. "That's so sweet."

She had meant the game to be a fun way to get to know each other, not something to bring up heartache.

"It's all right, Tess. I like remembering her. Thank you," Luke said.

He shook the memory free and straightened in his chair. "Okay, my turn."

Tessa steeled herself emotionally. She wasn't much of a sharer, so she hoped he would go easier on her. But for some reason? Luke was slowly becoming a person she could finally open up to.

Luke watched as Tessa's shoulders tightened. She looked like she was about ready to go into battle. *Okay, so no childhood memories for her today*, he thought. This was all about fun and relaxation.

"What do you do to help yourself feel better after a re-ally bad day? What brings Tessa back from the brink of a meltdown?"

Tessa blinked at his question. *She was definitely expect-ing something deeper*, Luke thought with a chuckle.

"Oh…uh…well, can you keep a secret?"

She leaned forward and her eyes had a mischievous sparkle in them. His stomach flipped in a way that made him think he would promise this woman anything if she asked.

"Sure, I can. Just call me Fort Knox."

She held her hand up to her mouth to whisper conspiratorially, "I have a secret stash of chocolate in my room that none of the kids know about. I call it my 'emergency supply.'"

He laughed. "I think that is awesome. Anything else help you relax at home?"

Tessa shrugged. "Vanilla candles, I guess. I love their smell. But most of mine have all been used up."

He was sure it had happened a long time ago, and that Tessa had used all her resources on the kids and not wanted to spend anything on herself, even to purchase a new candle.

It reminded him that he was on a mission to show this girl a good time today. "You ready? Time for the next stop on the list."

Tessa sat up excitedly. "The bookstore?"

Luke grinned. "I've never seen anyone so excited about visiting one, but yes, that's where we will head next."

They walked down the street toward the small independent bookshop in town. His fingers brushed against Tessa's, and he fought the urge to grab her hand in his. Why had the urge even crossed his mind?

Her bounce of excitement as they entered the bookstore pulled him from his thoughts. Luke had definitely done the right thing by bringing her here. She went up and down the aisles, running her fingers along the spines of several books.

"Pick out a couple, on me."

She gasped. "Oh, no, I couldn't. You've already done so much for me."

Luke waggled a finger at her. "This fun day is my treat. I'm the one who insisted on you having it, so it's only fair that I should pay."

Tessa opened her mouth to object again but stopped when he folded his arms across his chest.

"This is one of those things you're going to be stubborn about, isn't it?" she asked. The way that she talked to him, it felt like they had been friends for years rather than days.

"Absolutely."

To his surprise, she grinned up at him. "Well then, I'm not going to complain, because I have been dying to get some new books to read."

What Luke hadn't expected was that it would take her practically forever to pick out just a few to take home. Not that he was bored or anything. For some reason, watching Tessa fawn over books might become his new favorite pastime. She even started talking to them, which was kind of adorable.

"I'm sorry, I can't take all of you home. But I'll come back for you," she said wistfully as she carried a stack of three books to the counter. Luke grabbed one that she had put back with a sign and added it to her pile.

"Do you normally talk to books?"

She laughed. "They all want to come home with me."

Luke arched a brow at that. "Oh, really?"

Tessa nodded. "I have a big house, Luke. Lots of room for books. And kids."

He snorted as he handed his debit card to the clerk. "I have a feeling building a bookshelf might be added to the list of my handyman chores in the future."

Tessa took her bag from the clerk and did a little spin. "I can't thank you enough. I haven't had this much fun in... well, I can't remember when."

Luke was thrilled that he could do this for her, especially since she gave so much of herself to others.

"Okay, we do need to tackle some stuff on my to-do list," she said, holding up her hand when he started to protest. "I promise you that I'm not feeling guilty for having fun. I just really have to get some of that done."

He pulled both lists out of his pocket. "Okay, one more fun thing, and then we'll tackle all your errands. Choose wisely."

Tessa took her time looking over the list, weighing each fun task before finally pointing to one toward the bottom. "This one."

Luke squinted at the item. "You sure?"

She nodded, a wistful smile on her face. Ten minutes later, they had bags of seed they had purchased from the pet shop on the corner and entered the park. They headed straight for the pond.

"Why are you so fidgety?"

Tessa's question made him pause. "What? I'm not!"

"You totally are. Are you afraid of birds?"

Luke scoffed. "No way."

She pointed at him. "You totally are! How can a big brave fireman be afraid of some ducks?"

He shook his head. "It's not the ducks, it's the geese. I was chased by one as a kid."

Tessa burst out laughing but stopped when she saw that he wasn't. She held her hand out to him. "Come on, I'll protect you."

Thankfully, there were only ducks at the pond, and they

spent several restful minutes feeding the ones that hung out at the shore before the whole flock clued in that there was food and surrounded them. Laughing, they tossed handfuls of seed until they it was all gone and retreated to a nearby picnic table to watch the birds fight over the scraps.

"That was fun. What made you think to do that?" he asked.

A shadow flashed across her features. "My parents used to bring me here, before they died."

Luke wiped at the solitary tear running down her face. "I'm sorry. We should have done something different if it was going to make you sad."

She shook her head. "No, I'm glad we did. You talking about your mom reading that story reminded me that it's important to remember the good things about the people we've lost. Or we will get stuck just thinking about the fact that we lost them."

He nodded, feeling another wave of sympathy for her. He at least still had his dad after his mom had died. But Tessa? She had no one. She lost not only her parents but also life as she knew it.

Tessa seemed content to stay in silence for a while, before jumping back into the random-question game. "Okay, it's my turn again. You are so good with Tommy, so I know you'll make a great dad someday. How did you settle on the number of kids you want in this perfect life of yours that you've planned?"

She had a teasing look in her eyes, but not in a mean way.

"I've always thought two was a perfect number since that's what my family looked like. We didn't give my dad too much trouble," Luke said.

Tessa nodded, watching the lake. "So, not ten like me?"

The corner of her mouth ticked up. He could not imagine living in a house with ten kids at once. It sounded terrifying.

"I think that takes someone with a stronger constitution," he said.

She laughed. "Yeah, someone who is afraid of geese could never handle it."

"They are *mean*, Tess. Really," he said.

Tessa giggled and patted his shoulder. "There, there, it will be fine. Not all of us have the life goal nor the ability to parent ten kids at once."

He eyed her. "Yeah, it takes a special person."

She nudged him. "You're special too. But in a different way. Look how much you've done for me in such a short amount of time. You barely even know me."

Luke didn't think that was true anymore. He was starting to know Tessa very well, and he liked everything he learned about her.

But their conversation today about how many kids they wanted had proved what he had suspected all along—nothing could ever happen romantically between them. They didn't want the same things out of life.

Disappointment filled him, however, because this was the best day he'd had in a very long time. And it was funny—all the activities they did together had not been on his to-do list for the day either. His well-organized life had a little bit of chaos in it already, just by being her friend. Which meant they could never be anything more.

Chapter Eleven

Tessa hugged the weeping little girl in her lap, trying not to let her fuming rage show on her face. Little Emma was supposed to have had a visit with her biological parents today, but they hadn't shown up.

She had been a crying mess for the last hour. "Please tell me this is going in their file," Tessa had said to Sierra when the case worker told her the news.

"Absolutely," Sierra said, the cold rage barely contained in her voice. This was the toughest part of what they did—seeing these children suffer. Tessa gave most parents the benefit of the doubt because many of them were struggling and needed help in their own way, but she hated the toll it took on the kids who came into her care.

"Did I ever tell you about my parents?"

The little girl gave a big sniff and looked up at her with tear-filled eyes. "They died, right?"

Tessa nodded. "Yeah, but when they were alive, not everything was perfect. It's easy for me to try to remember them that way because they are gone, but they had some struggles, especially my dad."

Emma sat up and wiped at her face, smudging dirt and

tears together. Tessa made a mental note to get her set up with a relaxing bubble bath as soon as possible. "They did?"

Tessa pulled up the little girl so that she was sitting in front of her and started braiding her hair—something she remembered her mom doing to comfort her in childhood.

"Yeah, my dad worked a lot of hours. He was gone on business a lot. I was really small at the time, and I remember them fighting. He would just storm out of the house and leave for days, weeks at a time."

Her stomach soured at the memory. She would rather think about her father fondly, but connecting with Emma was more important.

"Did you miss your daddy?"

Tessa sighed. "I sure did. And I wondered all the time if it was my fault that he was gone. Was I too naughty? Did I cost too much money for food and stuff, and that's why he had to work so much? Did mommy fight with him because she was mad at me too?"

Emma's body stiffened. "Sometimes I feel like that too. Like I was bad and that's why I got taken away. That's why they don't want to visit."

Tessa fought back tears as she leaned forward and kissed the little girl's forehead. "Sweet girl, this is not your fault at all. You were not bad. Nothing you could ever have done could have changed what happened to your family."

Emma let out a shuddered sob. "You sure?"

Tessa tilted the girl's face up so their eyes could connect. "I'm positive, sweetie. My momma told me this, too, one day when she braided my hair just like this."

"What did she say?"

"She said that we can't control how other people act, only ourselves. People in our lives are going to be mean or bad sometimes, but we are in charge of how we react to it. My dad and your parents…they made some bad choices. They didn't react well to the problems in their lives. That is their fault, not ours."

Tessa cringed at her words, hoping Emma wouldn't think she was calling her a problem. "I just mean that grown-ups are supposed to be the ones who can provide some control. It is not your fault if they can't. It's theirs."

She explained that grown-ups need therapy, too, just how they see Miss Sophia once a week at her house. "Your parents need help, but they don't have the same people in their lives to provide that for them."

Emma nodded. "Like you and Miss Sierra."

Tessa resumed her braiding. "Exactly. Your parents love you very much, but they aren't able to make good choices. Hopefully, someone helps them learn to do that, but until that happens, you're going to have to stay with me or another foster parent, because what is the number one rule?"

"Kids need to be safe," the both of them said at the same time.

Tessa kissed her cheek. "That's right, sweetie. You are safe. You are loved. And it's going to be okay, even when it feels like it isn't."

Tessa grabbed hair ties and secured the girl's braids. "There are so many people in this world who love you. And sometimes love isn't just about blood, like who you are related to. Sometimes it's about who grows in your heart. You've grown in mine, sweet girl."

She finished the girl's hair and Emma leaped into her arms. "Thank you, Tessa. I love you."

Tessa squeezed her tight. "I love you too, sweetie. Now, what else do we do when we have a sad day?"

Emma jumped up. "We make cookies!"

Tessa grinned. "Absolutely. You go inside and gather all the ingredients. I'll be with you in a minute."

Once the little girl was gone, she let her face fall into her hands and wept. No matter how much she tried to hide it, sometimes what these kids went through reminded her so much of her own childhood. The times when she felt alone and scared. As if no one in the world could love her.

Sometimes, she still felt alone, but that was why she loved having a house full of kids. She never really would be. And she could be there for them in a way very few were for her. Emma's parents would either turn themselves around or she would be placed with a forever family that would love her the way she deserved. In the meantime, Tessa was going to do all she could to make sure that child knew her worth.

"Hey, are you all right?"

Tessa almost groaned at the man asking the question. The last thing she needed was for Luke to see her cry.

"I'm fine."

He plopped down next to her. "Tess, you don't have to put on a brave face. Not for me. I heard the conversation you had with Emma."

She narrowed her eyes at him. "That was meant to be private."

Luke put up his hands in surrender. "It was an accident, I promise. I just… I'm sorry you had things so rough even before you went into foster care. I didn't know that."

Tessa wiped tears from her face. "Yeah, well, there's a lot you don't know about me."

He gave her a rueful smile. "I know a lot about you, Tessa Duncan. The number one thing is that you are taking the pain you went through and turning it into something beautiful here with these kids."

Tessa let out a huffing laugh. "You don't know that I do it for selfish reasons. I didn't have a family, so I made a way so I would never be alone."

He studied her for a moment. "Yeah, but you do it for the kids too. The fact that you have the company is just a bonus for you, isn't it?"

She shrugged and he bumped shoulders with her. "I've seen you sacrifice everything of yourself for this place. That's not selfish at all."

Tessa sighed. "I just don't want them to have the same experiences as I did."

"See? You are a blessing to those kids. And God is using your past to help you be the exact person they need in their lives when they are going through the scariest things. That's why this place is so important."

Her eyes filled with tears again, though not from sadness this time. He got it. Finally, someone understood why she was doing all this. "And they need to open others like this place. I've been talking to a few other people who were kids in care the same time as me…and they are interested in opening homes too. If we get the green light and funding from the state."

She hadn't told anyone yet, not even Sierra, that she had people lined up to open the new homes. Tessa didn't want to count her chickens before they were hatched. But she trusted Luke.

"That's amazing," he said, holding up his arms. "See? I've got goose bumps from just hearing about this news. The guys and I are going to do everything in our power to fix up this house so you knock the socks off those inspectors."

Tessa was at a loss for words that there was now someone who believed in her mission almost as much as she did. She was going to open her mouth and tell him so when a loud banging noise sounded from upstairs, followed by screams from the children.

"Why do your children start screaming from some catastrophe every time we sit down to have a conversation?" Luke teased.

This was becoming quite the tradition. "Well, to be fair, they scream other times too. So the chances are always high that we'll be interrupted."

He snorted. "Excellent point. Come on, let's go see what we can rescue them from now."

Tessa couldn't help but smile as she followed Luke into the house. It didn't matter what disaster awaited them when they entered the house. At least she had someone to face it with.

Catastrophe was indeed the word Luke would use to describe the situation they discovered upstairs. When the guys were fixing the bathroom, a pipe burst and water was getting everywhere. Children were running around, screaming and soaking wet. Some of the kids were sprinting through the water on purpose and laughing while harried-looking volunteers tried to grab them.

"What happened?" Luke asked as he was handed a drenched two-year-old to pass to Tessa on the stairs. The woman in question was looking at the situation with a mix of fear and devastation that he wanted to wipe away immediately.

"This is an old house. And once we got in to work on some of the plumbing, it messed with other things. We need to get them all out of here and figure out what to do. Dean went down to turn off the water supply," Tom explained.

Tessa let out a whimper. "We need water—you can't shut it off."

He placed a hand on her shoulder. "It will just be until we can fix it, Tess. Get the kids out to the yard, and we'll see if we can get you some answers."

Judging from the mess and the water damage Luke could already see, it wasn't going to be pretty. There was no way Tessa and the kids could sleep here tonight. That was a problem for a little bit later. First, they had to figure out the status of the house.

The flowing water finally shut off, and they all breathed a sigh of relief. But it was short lived when they saw the absolute mess the house was in. Tom whistled. "This is going to be a lot of work."

Luke nodded. "We can do it. Well, I'm going to do it—I don't want to speak for you guys."

"Oh, stop. You know we're all here to help. Even Sam said he would try to make it over a few nights this week. If we get all hands on deck, we can get this all cleaned up and done in time," Tom said.

Luke surveyed the damage. "This is bigger than any job we've done before."

But the experience would be good for them. And it was for an amazing cause. "Let's get a plumber out here to fix the pipes, because I think that's out of our skill set."

Finn whistled. "That's going to cost a pretty penny."

It would, but Luke was sure the church would take up a collection, and he could chip in some of his savings. He had meant what he said to Tessa about making sure this place would look impressive for the state inspectors. They would just have to work a little harder now.

"I'll call my dad and others in his retirement crew to come help too," Luke said. "Then maybe they can help us with some of the smaller things while we rip up this carpet and replace it with something else."

He looked around the hallway, which featured old Victorian wallpaper and a faded-green carpet. "We can make this place a little more kid friendly."

The other men agreed and set to work on their various tasks. Luke took a moment to make all the phone calls he needed to before he went downstairs to talk to Tessa. He wanted to make sure he had everything taken care of to ease her worries.

Luke didn't know why he expected her to be wringing her hands with anxiety—Tessa was staying strong for the kids. She and the other volunteers were organizing games in the yard to keep all the little ones occupied.

Laughter filled the air, a stark contrast to the stress that had dampened the mood just ten minutes ago. When Tessa made eye contact with him, she separated from the group.

"Well, how bad is it?"

Luke wasn't one to lie or sugarcoat things, so he gave it to her straight: "It's pretty bad. The floors are damaged, and some of the walls and cabinets. We have fans coming from everyone's house to dry things out before we get started on ripping out what needs to go."

Tessa winced. "Was it just in the bathroom and hallway?"

"No, it seeped under the doors into most of the bedrooms too."

She groaned and rubbed her temples. "I guess I'm going to have to start calling hotels and see if they can fit me and ten kids for the night. And then Sierra is going to have to find new homes for them."

Luke's eyebrows furrowed. "What do you mean? These kids belong with you."

"I don't have a home to keep them in," Tessa said. "They need to have a roof over their head. I can't give them that right now."

"Take my place," he blurted out without thought. But he didn't regret it. He had a whole house just sitting there, empty except for him and his dog. She might as well put it to good use.

"What?" Tessa was staring at him with narrowed eyes. "I can't just take your house. You live there."

Luke shrugged. "I also have a bunk at the fire station. I'll just camp out up there for the few weeks it takes to get this place fixed up and approved by the state."

Tessa was already shaking her head. "We're going to have to cancel that inspection. There is no way we are going to be able to fix up this mess in time, let alone all the other fixes that needed to be made."

"O ye of little faith. That's exactly what we're going to do. I have a plan," Luke said.

Tessa bit her lip, her attention darting between the loud kids playing in the yard, an older woman holding Tommy and Luke. "We'll mess up your house. I'm sure you have it all neat and organized."

He did. And he was sure the kids would indeed throw it all into chaos. But he didn't really care. He wouldn't be living there for a couple of weeks to see it, anyway. And this was more important than his need for organization.

"It will just give me some fun projects to do when all this is settled."

Tessa smirked. "Well, you do love organizing things."

"You know it."

Her shoulders dropped, resigned. "All right. If you're sure. I'll call Sierra and have her run over and do an emergency inspection and approval for the kids to be moved to that house instead of this one. I may have to make some changes to make it kid friendly."

Luke grinned. "Well, that's totally fine with me. I wanted to be a father someday, right? Now I'll just be one step ahead of the game."

Tessa reached out and grabbed his hand. The warmth of her touch immediately chased out the chill that was setting in with the oncoming evening. "Luke, seriously, though. I can't thank you enough for this. You just keep giving and giving. I don't understand it."

The older woman holding Tommy brought him over to them, and Luke scooped his favorite little guy up into his arms. The baby wrapped his fingers around the cloth of Luke's shirt.

"I do it so this guy can have the best home possible. I do it because you deserve to have help in your mission here. I do it because you are not alone, Tessa. You have people that care about you too. Remember what you said to Emma about family earlier? It's more than blood."

As he said the words, a peace settled into Luke as he realized they were true. Tessa, Zack, Tommy, Emma, the other kids, the church volunteers, his crew… They were all family in their own way. The baby had created an opening in his heart, and the rest of them had filled it with so much more.

This all may not be part of his life plan, but he wasn't sure he would trade it for anything in the world.

Chapter Twelve

❦

"I can't believe he's giving you a whole house," Sierra said as Tessa unlocked the door to Luke's place.

She felt along the wall next to the entryway for the lights. "He's not giving it to me. I'm just borrowing it for a while."

Sierra snorted. "Give, borrow... Either way, this is huge of him."

Both of them blinked as the room illuminated. Tessa grinned as she took in the modern, clean, organized home. Just what she would have expected from Luke. "Oh, the kids are going to destroy this place."

Sierra agreed. "But at least they will have a fun time doing it. Wasn't he supposed to meet us here?"

Tessa nodded. "Yeah, he had to get a few more things handled at the house. I dropped the kids off at the church, and they are getting entertained by the volunteers there until we get everything here set up."

The two walked around the house, noting things that might need to be made child-proof before the kids arrived. Despite its lack of vibrant colors and lived-in clutter, Luke's place still felt warm and welcoming. *Just like him*, Tessa thought. She frowned. Was she becoming too attached to the man?

There were picture frames featuring Luke, his sister and her family, and their father. The couch featured pillows and cozy blankets. He had a giant TV and a video game system her older kids would go crazy for.

"Let's go upstairs and look at the bedrooms," Sierra said. There were only three, which would make this whole thing a tight fit, but Tessa planned on sleeping on the couch, and the baby and the youngest of the toddlers had cribs. They could make it work. She let out a giggle when she saw how neatly Luke's closet was organized.

"He really likes everything to be in order, doesn't he?" Sierra tapped at the man's shoes, which were put in order of function and color.

At first, Tessa found it frustrating and annoying, but now, after she had gotten to know Luke…it was kind of endearing. "Some people just like things a certain way. He lets loose when he needs to."

Sierra's eyebrow arched at her defense of him. "You two have gotten pretty close."

Tessa nodded. "Yes, he's becoming a really good *friend*."

She emphasized the last word, hoping that Sierra would get the point. She and Luke may get along great, but their life choices were far too different to be compatible in any other way than friends.

"I don't know… Friends don't lend their spotless houses to other friends who have ten kids," the case worker argued.

Tessa lifted her chin. "He's a good man."

Luke was probably one of the sweetest men she had ever met. Thankfully, Sierra let the subject drop.

"Did you bring the supplies you need?"

Tessa dumped out a plastic bag filled with all the extra

child-proofing supplies she had at her house. Sierra's phone buzzed, and she frowned as she looked down at it.

"I have to go do an emergency kid pickup. Once Luke gets here, you guys get started doing everything on the checklist, and I'll come back to inspect it and give you temporary approval for this place."

Tessa nodded. "Thanks for being so flexible with us."

Her friend waved her hand. "Please, this actually saves me a lot of time because finding a home for ten kids at the last minute would be a nightmare. Especially when they have someone as great as you to look after them."

Tessa's cheeks burned. Once she was alone in the house, she got to work putting plastic protectors in each of the electrical sockets she could find around the house.

"I see you're making yourself at home," Luke said from behind her while she was leaning over and trying to get to one on the other side of the couch. He startled her so much that she yelped and toppled over on the floor. She banged her elbow on the side table on the way down.

"You scared me half to death!"

Luke looked apologetic and immediately moved to inspect her injury. "Let me go get you an ice pack from the freezer."

"I'm fine, really."

He shook his head. "If you have an injury in a firefighter's house and don't get first aid…that should be a crime or something."

Tessa giggled at that and waited patiently while he got the ice pack and held it up to her elbow.

"I think you'll be okay, Miss Duncan, but no more flying leaps off couches in the future, please," Luke said in a professional voice.

Tessa bit her lip to keep from laughing. "I will, sir. Thank you for your service."

They sat there with him holding the ice to her elbow for a few moments. Their eyes locked. She noticed that he had little laugh lines starting to appear on the sides of his face—a clear sign he was living a happy life. Even if it was one he had planned down to every detail. She had a strange urge to reach out and touch those lines, but she shook her head and pulled away from him. They had a task here to do.

"I…uh…think that I got these in all your sockets. Do you have a drill?"

He arched a brow. "You're going to put holes in my wall?"

Tessa winced. "Not your wall. Just your cupboards. You have cleaning supplies under every sink. So either we have to put a lock on all your cupboards or you have to take all the supplies and put them in a closet and keep that locked up. Plus, I have to keep all their medications locked up. Foster parent–safety rules."

A wave of guilt ran through her again; she was making him change stuff in his house to accommodate her. "I'm sorry, I know this is a lot."

"Tess, it's fine. I expect that you would have to do stuff like this. If I hadn't wanted to, I wouldn't have offered for all of you to stay here. Let's keep working on kid-proofing my place," Luke said.

He ended up putting a lock on every single cabinet that was under a sink and on a closet in the hallway so she could store meds in there. He even turned down the temp on the water heater so the kids wouldn't accidentally turn it on too high and burn themselves.

"Are we missing anything else?" he asked.

Tessa looked at the list. Just about everything was done, except one thing. "I assume, given your career, that we don't have to go out and buy a fire extinguisher at the last minute?"

Luke chuckled. "There are two on each floor."

She laughed. "Then I think we are all good. I can't wait to get the kids here and settled in."

They made a trip back to her house with his truck and grabbed the cribs and toddler beds, and as much bedding that wasn't soaked from the pipe incident as they could. Someone in the church had loaned them some camping cots to make extra beds for the older kids.

She and Luke worked together for the next hour or so, getting it all set up.

"I think that will do for the night," she said. "They have to be exhausted since they've been playing at the church for so long and they had that excitement from earlier."

Luke grinned. "Let's go get them, then!"

Tessa laughed at his eagerness. "You don't have to go with me. I have my sixteen-passenger van and can drive them all myself."

He pulled the keys out of her hand. "Well, that means you have room for the both of us."

Tessa was right—the kids were very tired when they picked them up. But they were displaying it by being hyper and crabby. The whole way back to Luke's house was filled with whining and arguing. He winced when baby Tommy's cry hit a particularly high note.

"Are you regretting coming with me?"

His lips quirked up. "Strangely, no."

Luke looked just as confused about that as she felt. He

was a bachelor, used to an organized, quiet life. And yet here he was, thriving in the chaos.

Sierra was in the driveway when they got back. Once the kids were in and settled, the case worker did her inspection of the home and declared it ready. Luke agreed to put a movie on the giant TV, and soon all her kids were curled up on his living room floor or on his big sectional sofa.

"I bought that for game days with the guys," he whispered. "I never knew it would come in handy someday."

He declared he was going out to grab them all some dinner, and he was out the door before she could even protest that she could make something or offer him money to help pay for it. Tessa didn't think he had any idea just how much pizza for ten hungry kids and two adults could cost.

Luke's wallet was hurting when he got back to the house, but he was pleased with his purchase. "Who wants pizza?" he called out when he opened the door, and was greeted with gleeful shouts from the kids.

Tessa was looking at the stack of pizza boxes in his hands with trepidation. "Don't worry," he said, giving a gentle poke to the frown line between her brows. "I bought some that met the allergy requirements. There is a gluten-free one. And a dairy-free one."

She blinked at him in surprise. "You remembered?"

"Of course I did. I wouldn't want anyone to get sick on my watch," Luke said.

He set out the pizza boxes on the counter and made each kid line up according to which one they could eat. Tessa handed out plates, all the while sneaking looks at him.

"What?" he finally asked. Her scrutiny was making him

nervous that he had done something wrong. "Did I miss an allergy?"

She shook her head. "No, I just can't believe you had all of them memorized. It's made me wonder…"

"What?"

"Well…" She hesitated. "I know you have a perfect plan for exactly how life should go. And how everything should be in its place but…it seems to me that your attention to detail and organization makes you the perfect person to handle a wild bunch like this."

She waved a hand at the kids, who were eating happily. "I know you have plans otherwise, but I think you should maybe try to become a foster father. You're great with kids."

He was silent for a moment before deciding to tell her about his previous conversation with Sierra. "I asked about the possibility of getting approved to adopt Tommy."

Tessa's entire face brightened. "That's so amazing! I knew the two of you were meant to be a family. And look, with this inspection that Sierra did, you're one step closer to getting approved."

Her enthusiasm for what wasn't meant to be made his heart ache even more. "No, she said the list of couples waiting for a baby was really long. And that the state is more likely to place with them than with a single dad."

Tessa gave a disgruntled scowl. "Well, that's just ridiculous. Tommy is already bonded to you, and it is best that he be with someone he already has an attachment with."

He shrugged, throwing up his arms in resignation. "We're not the bosses of the system. Besides, that's just a sign from God that it's not meant to be. I really want Tommy to be in the best home for him."

She sighed. "I still think that's with you. And if you've

taught me anything, it's that you can't give up. God will surprise you."

Luke arched a brow at that. "I haven't heard you talk much about your faith before."

"I haven't really been that much of a church person. But over the past few weeks, with everything going on with the inspection... I've really found peace in turning to Him. Besides, the people in your church really make it hard to be skeptical of their intent to be kind to people," Tessa said.

He laughed. "Yeah, they kind of love people without much regard for boundaries. We're working on that with them."

She swatted at his chest. "Don't you dare. Who knows what they might do for someone else down the road who doesn't realize they needed help until a whole group of senior citizens shows up at their door with cleaning supplies?"

The two of them shared a laugh, and a meal as they ate the "adult" pizza he pulled out from the bottom of the stack. It was topped with vegetables, which the kids took one look at and declared "disgusting."

Luke helped Tessa with dinner, wondering if he was overstaying his welcome. He knew that she would insist that he couldn't do that in his own home, but it was technically hers and the kids' home for now.

"Do you want to put Tommy down and then do a story time with some of the kids? They insist that you will do a much better job at character voices than me," Tessa said, her tone full of mock indignation.

"I am an amazing big bad wolf," he proclaimed, thrilled she had asked him to stay.

Luke took little Tommy up to the room that had been set aside for the babies. He fed him a bottle, glad that they had also grabbed the rocking chair from Tessa's home. There was just something about sitting in it with Tommy that soothed the both of them. Sure that Tessa and the kids were busy downstairs, he sang a lullaby his mom used to sing to him.

Tommy was out by the end of the first chorus, but Luke kept rocking and singing. Finally, he kissed the baby's head and laid him down in the crib. "I wish I could have been your dad," he whispered. "But I'll always be there for you, whenever you need it."

He snuck out of the room, surprised to see Tessa standing there. "I thought you were putting the others to bed."

She smiled at him. "I was waiting for you to finish up so I could put the other littlest ones in there."

Luke had forgotten that all the kids three and younger were sharing a room. "Ah, sorry about that."

She put up her hands. "No need to apologize, I was enjoying your song. I remember it from when I was little."

He felt his cheeks warm. "Me too."

"And I heard what you said to Tommy. I still think you're going to be his dad. You just have to have faith."

Luke felt frustration fill him. "I'm not even trying anymore. It's not meant to be. I just asked about it, just in case it was a possibility. It isn't, so I won't pursue it. End of story."

Tessa gave him a sad smile. "Okay. I'm sorry, I'll drop it."

He felt bad for lashing out at her, but the entire subject had made him a little touchy. "It's okay. I'm just…tired, I guess."

"Do you want me to tell the bedtime story instead?"

He snorted. "No way—I promised. And besides. I don't want to traumatize the kids with your horrible acting."

"You're so rude."

"I bought you pizza. And remembered allergies."

"Okay, you're nice with periodic bouts of rudeness."

They stood there in the hallway grinning at each other until one of the toddlers ran up to them, squeezing both their legs. "I no go to sweep!"

Tessa laughed and scooped the little one up. "Not an option, princess. Let's get you tucked in, and I'll sing you your favorite song."

Luke was tempted to wait around and listen to her sing. But he had a bedtime story to tell.

An hour later, when he was finally alone in his truck on the way back to the station, the quiet that he usually craved made him feel...lonely.

Chapter Thirteen

❧

The next day, Luke was at the house again with a truck full of groceries to help feed the kids. He knocked, and Zack answered the door in his pajamas.

"Why are you knocking at your own house?"

Luke shrugged. "Because I don't live here at the moment—you guys do."

The boy's face crinkled. "Still seems weird to me."

Luke ruffled his hair and pointed to the truck. "You wanna help me carry groceries in? I bought pancake mix."

That was the exact right thing to say, because Zack was pulling on his shoes and running to grab an armful of bags.

Tessa looked up from the bottles of formula she was making in the kitchen when they set the bags on the counter.

"Groceries were on my to-do list today," she said.

Luke winked. "Well, you can cross that one off. I really didn't have a lot in the pantry, so I figured you would need supplies for breakfast."

Tessa nodded. "I did grab a few things from my house, but yes, a store run was going to be necessary."

He and Zack began making pancakes while Tessa fed Tommy his bottle. "Are you sure you don't want to switch and do this? I know you love to."

Luke shook his head. "Nah, I promised this guy we could make these together."

He nudged Zack, and the boy grinned as he mixed all the ingredients. "We're going to try to flip them higher than last time."

Luke only hoped he wouldn't end up with pancakes on the ceiling. Breakfast was a wild and fun affair, with kids eating at the table, in the living room or pretty much anywhere they could find a seat. Tessa fretted that they would get syrup on his furniture. A valid concern, but Luke found that he didn't care for some reason.

After they ate, the older kids attacked the video games while the little ones ran around the house in a game of hide-and-seek. There hadn't been this much noise in his home…ever. Luke could not wipe the smile from his face.

"Please stop running, you guys," Tessa called as they did a lap through the kitchen.

"They're just being kids."

She wrung her hands. "Yeah, but sometimes in being a kid…you can break something by accident. Luke, this was a bad idea. They are definitely going to destroy your stuff."

He waved a hand. "It's just stuff. There's nothing here that can't be replaced."

Tessa didn't look any less concerned. Luke wanted to put her at ease. "Why does this have you so worried?"

She sighed. "Well, we just started being friends. And you've done so much for me, Harmony House and for the kids… I'm just nervous that something will get broken and you'll get mad, and it would ruin our friendship."

Luke froze at her words. Where on earth would she get that idea? "Have I gotten angry with you or the kids since you met me?"

Even when they had drenched him with water, he stayed calm, and had turned it into a big water fight.

Tessa shrugged. "I know. That's not you. I guess you can say that this is just carryover anxiety I have from my childhood."

Luke's jaw tightened. "Did one of your foster families get mad at you for breaking something?"

She nodded. "Yeah, and I got sent to another home. One time, it was another kid that did it, but I took the blame and got moved again. It wasn't long before I was labeled a problem and it was harder and harder to place me."

Anger filled Luke's veins. How could people treat children like that? Tessa had just been someone they could discard when they were mad?

He reached across the counter and grabbed her hand. "I'm sorry they did that to you, but I wouldn't be mad it they broke something. And even if they did, you're not getting rid of me. In fact, you will get to the point when you wish you could."

Tears filled her eyes. "Okay, I'll try to remember that."

It was interesting to see this strong, driven woman share something that gave her anxiety. His admiration for him grew.

"Um… Mr. Luke?" came a shaky voice from the doorway of the kitchen. Chase, age five, was standing there with something behind his back.

"What's going on, buddy?"

He moved his arms forward to reveal that he was holding the pieces of a broken vase. The one from his living room. Luke did a quick once-over of the boy to make sure he didn't have any cuts. "Did anyone get hurt?"

Chase shook his head, his eyes closed as if waiting for Luke to scream at him.

"I guess my concerns are being put to the test immediately," Tessa murmured under her breath.

Luke burst into laughter, a big and booming from his belly.

"What's so funny?" Chase asked defensively. "Why are you laughing at me?"

Luke hurried to put the boy at ease. "I'm not laughing at you, just the situation. Don't worry about it, kid. I didn't like that vase much anyway."

Tessa shot him a grateful look and hurried after Chase with a broom and dustpan to clean up any glass pieces that might have broken free. Luke was surprised at how little he cared about the vase.

He looked around his kitchen, which had been clean and kind of sterile yesterday. It was now filled with clutter everywhere. Kids' drawings were now on the refrigerator.

This house feels like a home for the first time, he thought. *There's life in it.*

And for some reason, he doubted things around here would ever be the same again.

Tessa was just finishing the last of the breakfast dishes when a knock sounded at the backdoor.

"Grandpa's here," a booming voice came from the other side.

"No, I'm the grandpa too," said another voice.

"We're all the grandpas. You should have said 'All the grandpas are here.' Then they would know there was more than one."

The first man gave a disgruntled noise. "It doesn't matter how I word it. I just wanted to get the kids excited."

Tessa didn't know who was behind the door, but they were making her smile. She opened the door to see men with silver hair having an intense discussion. Based on the photographs on the walls of this house, she recognized one of them as Luke's father.

"Hello, would you all like to come in?"

The group stopped their banter to give her beaming smiles. Each one of them introduced themselves, and the one named Thomas was indeed the dad of their host.

"Luke has told me so much about you and what you've been doing for those kids. I just had to come down and see them all for myself," he said. He introduced Robert and William, his pickleball buddies.

"We usually hit the courts every week at this time, but we wanted to come over and be granddads to these kids. We heard some of the ladies at church were becoming honorary grandmas, and we want in on the action," Thomas said.

Tessa chuckled. This town really did have some sweet people in it. "Well, the more people who want to care for these kids, the better. Do you want some coffee?"

She poured them all a cup while the men discussed what being a grandfather meant. Advice, cool stories, and peppermint and butterscotch candies were the lead categories, though they each agreed that the kids needed some extra spoiling from them as well.

"My back isn't what it used to be, but I can still do piggyback rides," Robert said.

"And I can definitely play catch and attend some tea parties," William chimed in.

Tessa beamed at them. "I'm sure the kiddos would love that."

Luke wandered downstairs after putting Tommy down for a nap, and he didn't seem surprised to see his father there. "I knew it was only a matter of time until you showed up."

Thomas gave his son a hug, and Tessa let herself wish for a moment that she had a parent to care for her even as an adult.

As if he'd read her thoughts, Thomas turned to Tessa and pulled her in for a hug. "Now I am going to be an extra grandfather to these kids, that means I get to adopt you as well."

He pulled papers out of his wallet and handed them over. "We had our background checks done too. And we contacted Sierra to get approval to watch the kids. We wanna spoil you too."

Thomas nudged Luke in the ribs. "Ask the lovely lady out to a nice lunch while we take care of the kids."

Luke grunted at the nudge. "I have to work on the other house today. We have a lot to get done."

His father narrowed his eyes at him. "You can spare an hour or two to take Tessa to lunch. She will love the quiet and adult conversation."

Tessa's hand covered her mouth to hold in her laugh at the sight of Luke's father messing with his plans for the day. "He doesn't have to take me out. He's already done enough for me."

Luke frowned at that. "I would love to take you to lunch. I just didn't want you to think I was slacking on the other stuff. We can grab a meal before I head over to do some work. I want to get as much done as possible before my next two-day shift."

Why was everyone being so nice to her? This was an entirely new experience for Tessa, and she had no idea how to handle it.

"But you guys are just meeting the kids. They might not want to be with strangers—"

She cut off her objection because the three older men were already playing with the kids. One was trying his hand at video games while Zack tried to explain it to him. Another was offering piggyback rides and getting his hair pulled by Emma. Thomas was reading a book with the toddlers around him, in rapt attention.

"How did they get over there so fast?"

Luke smirked. "They are in great shape. It's the pickleball."

Tessa giggled. "Well, I had better sign up, then."

"With all your free time."

The teasing glint in his eyes made little butterflies twirl around in Tessa's stomach. She looked down at the raggedy sweatpants and T-shirt she was wearing. "I, uh, have to go change before we go."

He told her to take all the time she needed, but she still raced up the stairs to find something decent to wear. She really hadn't packed much that would suffice, but she finally settled on a yellow dress with white flowers on it that always made her feel pretty. She tied her hair up in a loose bun and studied herself in the mirror.

She still had circles under her eyes, but she looked passable enough for a lunch with a handsome fireman. *It's not a date*, she told herself. *Don't get yourself all worked up.*

Tessa and Luke were just friends, and that's all they

ever could be. But that didn't mean she couldn't enjoy a lunch out with him. Luke gave her a smile of approval when she walked back into the kitchen, which made her cheeks turn pink.

Get yourself together, Tessa. This man is doing a lot for you and your kids. You owe him more than to crush on him like a schoolgirl.

"You ready?"

She eyed the kids in the living room, feeling a little guilty for leaving them with their new "grandpas."

"Remember, it's okay to accept help, Tessa," Luke teased.

"I know, I know. So you keep telling me."

They decided on lunch at the little Mexican restaurant in town. Most of their time was spent daring each other to taste increasingly hotter levels of sauce and laughing at the faces they made. As it turned out, Tessa had stronger taste buds than Luke.

"You know, I could insert some jokes here about how a firefighter should be able to handle heat better than me."

He laughed. "I appreciate your restraint."

As they finished their meal, Tessa thanked Luke again for loaning them his house. "I feel so bad that you're sleeping at the station every night. You don't need to go to work on your days off too."

He waved away her concern. "The beds there are comfier than you'd think. And I've worked there for a long time. It's like a second home to me now."

"Still…"

"Tess, please stop worrying about it. I'm happy that big house is finally being put to use by a family. I bought it for mine someday, and, well, that plan is taking longer than I expected," Luke said.

She knew he had a specific kind of woman in mind, but Tessa couldn't help but wonder why a kind and handsome man like Luke was single.

"Don't you date at all? It's hard to find your perfect woman when you aren't actively out there looking," Tessa asked.

Luke fidgeted in his seat. "I've gone out with a few women, but I haven't found…the one. You know?"

She nodded.

"What about you?"

Tessa laughed. "Like I said on the day we first met— I'm just happy if I can find someone who doesn't run away screaming when they hear I have ten kids at any given time."

Luke frowned. "They are foolish."

Tessa didn't know what to say to that. Her lifestyle was not for everyone. But it was hers, and she wouldn't change it for anything.

Tessa insisted that it was her turn to treat Luke to a meal, and she slipped her debit card to the waitress anyway when he protested.

"Well, thanks," he said as he opened the truck door for her. "I've got the next one."

She really hoped lunches would become a regular thing with him. Tessa could get used to all the fun she had been having lately.

"On the way home, can we stop at the thrift store? I want to get the kids some toys that aren't waterlogged. That way they don't destroy your home," Tessa said.

Luke pulled into the shop closest to the restaurant. "Why don't we both get a cart? That way we can get more."

Tessa arched a brow. "We don't need that many toys."

Only a few things to get them through the next couple of weeks would be fine. If she found a nice balance of indoor and outdoor toys, they should be set. Maybe some crafts.

Tessa felt the hair on the back of her neck start to rise. She had the strange sensation she was being watched. She looked around but didn't see anyone. All the changes in her life lately must have made her paranoid.

"We need to grab some more onesies for baby Tommy," she said. "He's been growing like a weed!"

Luke beamed proudly. "That's my boy—an over-achiever."

She snorted. "And all the bottles of milk we've been feeding him. He's such a sweet boy."

Tessa gasped. There it was again. The sensation. She turned around quickly, and this time she spotted a young woman peering at her from across the store.

"Luke…do you recognize that woman?"

He turned and his mouth dropped open. "That's her! The person at the church food drive who knew about Tommy."

The girl's eyes widened when Luke started walking in her direction. She turned and ran out the front of the store.

Tessa grabbed his arm. "Let me try to talk to her. I might be a softer approach."

He nodded and stopped walking. "Be careful."

Tessa ran out the front door and looked in every direction. It was a small town, so she could see down the main street in either direction. There wasn't really time for her to duck in another store, but she wasn't visible. Tessa guessed that she might be hiding near the building.

"Hello? Are you here?" she called out, hoping the girl could hear her. "You don't have to be afraid of me. I'm the one taking care of baby Tommy. That's what we named him for now. He's doing really well, and he's the sweetest baby. I know you are scared right now, but I can promise that you aren't in any trouble."

She waited for a moment, but she got no response. She reached into her purse and pulled out her card.

"I'm going to leave my contact information on this bench right here. When you feel comfortable enough to talk, I'll be there to listen."

She put the card down on the metal bench in front of the store, picking a rock off the ground to secure it so it wouldn't blow away.

Tessa waited another minute before sighing and heading inside.

"Did you find her?"

She shook her head. "No, she's just so scared." She told him about leaving her card.

He nodded thoughtfully. "I have a feeling this won't be the last we see of her. She wants to know what's going on with Tommy. We just have to give her time."

Tessa shrugged. "Let's hope she does reach out. In the meantime, we have some shopping to do."

Luke, it turned out, could not be trusted around toys. He put just about everything in the cart. And when Tessa returned them to the shelf, he snuck them right back into the cart again.

"You're such a big softie," she teased.

But she couldn't really fault him. It was great to see him so happy as he picked out the toys. The grin stayed on his face as they handed them out once they got home. The kids squealed over each and every one.

His smile didn't even fade when he got hit in the nose with a foam dart.

"I think you may regret some of those purchases," Tessa said.

"Never," he said as he joined the fray with the kids playing with the toys.

Tessa couldn't help but watch in amazement as the serious and put-together Luke Russell embraced his wild side.

Chapter Fourteen

The next week was a flurry of activity. Tessa was busy trying to keep the kids occupied and calm in their temporary home. She had tried to take on extra hours at work to help cover some of the costs for the repairs at her house, but the church took up a collection to cover it before she could.

Luke split his time between work, fixing the house and coming over to help the kids.

"I've never seen him this driven," Thomas said to Tessa one day as he observed his son teaching Zack how to kick a soccer ball. "You all have been good for him."

Tessa didn't know about that. They had kind of taken over Luke's life. He probably would enjoy some solace and alone time once this whole inspection thing was over. The thought of not seeing him every day didn't sit well with Tessa, but she wasn't going to borrow tomorrow's trouble.

Her phone buzzed in her pocket, and she frowned when she saw an unknown number. She seldom answered calls from people she didn't recognize, but she felt a strong pull to answer the phone. Tessa didn't think God would want her to talk to a scammer, so she trusted the feeling.

"Hello? This is Tessa Duncan."

There was silence on the other line.

"Hello? Is anyone there?"

More silence. She was about to hang up the phone when she heard a voice say, "Uh…hi."

"Hi! Who is this?"

Another beat, and then, "Lily."

"Are you the woman from the thrift store, Lily?"

"Y-yes," came a very faint reply.

"I'm so glad you called. I've been hoping to hear from you all week."

"You have?"

Tessa smiled into the phone. "Yes, I've been worried about you. Are you all right? Do you need anything?"

Lily sobbed slightly into the phone. "I'm okay. I got some food from the church. And clothes from the thrift store."

Tessa was thrilled the girl was gaining more confidence as they spoke. "That's great! I'm sorry that I scared you the other day. You're not in trouble."

"I know. I looked up the baby-drop thing. It's not illegal," Lily said defensively.

Tessa pulled out the dining room chair and sat down. Thomas had guessed that this was a serious conversation and was distracting the little ones. "You're right. You did the right thing. Are you Tommy's mother?"

Another sob sounded. "Yes. Well, not anymore, I suppose."

Tessa let out a tsk sound. "You're always going to be his mother, even if someone else is raising him. You were there when he was born. And you will be an important part of his life. In whatever way you choose."

A gasp sounded on the other line. "I can't choose to be in his life. I already gave him back."

Tessa waited a beat before asking the next question. "Do you...regret leaving him?"

This earned her a laugh. "No, not at all. I love Tommy— I like the name you gave him by the way—but I... I'm not ready to be a mother."

She sounded so sad and scared that it broke Tessa's heart. "That's all right. But that doesn't mean you have to stay away from him forever. You can still see him...if you want."

"I can?"

Tessa told the young woman that this conversation would be best had in person. "I have a babysitter coming this Thursday. Why don't we meet up for coffee and have a chat?"

To her surprise, the girl agreed.

"Would you mind if I brought Luke with me? The fireman who found Tommy in the baby drop at the station? He spends a lot of time with your son and can tell you all about him."

Tessa crossed her fingers that she would say yes. "I guess that would be all right."

They made the rest of the arrangements to meet, and Tessa got off the phone with Lily. She immediately dialed Luke and then Sierra to tell them the news.

She could hardly wait until Thursday. She felt like she was bouncing off the walls in anticipation. Tessa wanted to help Lily, and more importantly, she wanted the woman to have a chance to hold her son again.

On Thursday morning, Tessa dressed Tommy in his cutest onesie. Luke tucked the boy into the baby carrier he wore on his chest when he pulled him out of the car seat at the coffee shop.

"You think she's going to show?" he asked.

Tessa shrugged. "All we can do is hope and try to help her if she does. We have no control over whether she accepts that help."

They saw Lily waiting for them in front of the coffee shop, wringing her hands. Tessa hurried to set the young woman at ease. "Lily, hi. It's so good to see you."

She pulled Lily in for a hug, which she returned. Tessa wondered when the last time anyone had shown her affection was. "I'm Tessa. It's so nice to meet you. And this is Luke."

Lily eyed Luke suspiciously. He held out his hand to her, and she hesitated before shaking it.

"Lily, I'm glad you came. And I want to apologize for what I said about you throwing Tommy away the first time we met. It was out of line. I know that isn't what happened. I was just having a bad day, and I shouldn't have taken it out on you," Luke said.

She shook her head. "He's not trash, but I did give him away. So you weren't wrong about me."

He made eye contact with her and gave her a reassuring smile. "I'm sure you had your reasons. Why don't we grab something to drink and you can tell us all about it?"

Tessa noticed that Lily was looking everywhere but at Tommy. She wondered if it was too hard for her to see her son just yet. "How about Lily and I find a seat, and you and Tommy can put in our order?"

Luke winked at her and sauntered off, and Tessa guided Lily to a seat near the door. She wanted the woman to have a place to go if she felt the urge to run.

"You guys are so nice. I don't deserve it," Lily said tearfully.

"Of course you do," Tessa said, putting an arm around her. "Everyone deserves kindness."

"But I just gave up my baby! I left him there all alone. What kind of person doesn't want to be a mother?"

Tessa hugged the girl tighter. "You loved him enough to make sure he got put in a safe place where he would be taken care of when you couldn't. That is the best kind of mother."

Luke brought their drinks over one by one and finally sat across from them. "What did I miss?"

Tessa took a sip of her coffee, praying for guidance for the rest of this meeting. "I was just telling Lily that she did the right thing by Tommy by leaving him in a safe place."

Luke cupped the baby's head and nodded. "I agree. I've been on calls where mothers didn't make the same choice. Where babies were found in…unsafe conditions."

Lily's mouth dropped open. "Were they all right?"

A grim smile formed on his face. "Some were. Some weren't. Believe me when I tell you—you did right by this sweet boy."

Lily's eyes finally dropped to Tommy. "I did?"

Tessa smiled. "You really did. Do you want to hold him?"

Lily scooted back in her chair. "I'm not sure I'm ready for that."

"It's okay," she reassured Lily. "You don't have to."

The young woman's shoulders slumped in relief. "I suppose you want to hear about why I did it."

Luke and Tessa exchanged a glance. They did want to know, but they didn't want to pressure her and scare her away. "Only if you want to tell us."

Lily shrugged. "It will be good to get it off my chest."

She took a drink of her iced coffee before beginning.

"My boyfriend, Aiden, and I met in high school. He was going to sign up for the army right when we graduated. I would live on base with him, and we could start our lives right after high school."

Tessa nodded encouragingly.

"We eloped the moment I turned eighteen. My parents were furious because Aiden's family moved away, and it meant they had another mouth to feed until he had to report to the base for boot camp. And we wouldn't have another place to live until he got his first post."

Tessa's heart broke for the two young kids. Adults, but still so new to the world.

"And then when I got pregnant…it got so much worse. My parents kicked us out. We lived in a shelter for a while. I stayed there while Aiden went off to boot camp. I thought that if I could just survive on the streets until he graduated, it would all be okay."

Tears started filling Lily's eyes again, and Tessa passed her a tissue. "But it wasn't?"

Lily shook her head. "Aiden never came back. Not when he was supposed to, anyway. I called him and texted him every day, hoping he was all right. I was worried that the worst had happened to him. But then I got served with divorce papers. Aiden finally texted me to tell me that it was all too much for him to deal with now that he was starting his new life as a soldier. He had met someone else and would not be coming back for me and the baby. I was all alone with no home, and pregnant."

Luke shifted in his seat. "I'm so sorry that happened to you. Aiden was a coward, running away from his responsibilities."

Lily gave him a small smile. "Yeah, well, he had the opportunity to do so since he wasn't the one carrying the baby. I had fewer options. I was able to get into a crisis home for pregnant girls for the rest of the time I carried Tommy. They presented me with a lot of options, including how to set myself up to raise him. But…now I know that I rushed into being an adult too quickly. I'm not ready to be someone's mom. I need to figure myself out first."

Tessa nodded. "That makes a lot of sense."

"I knew it would be ultimately better for the baby if I put him in the safe-baby drop. I had seen a news story about it one time. I hoped he would get adopted and put in a new family."

Tessa squeezed her hand. "He will."

Lily eyed her son lovingly. "I'm so glad he's been with you. He looks like he's doing well. When I heard Luke talk about Tommy and then saw you in the thrift store buying baby clothes, I really just wanted to hear more about how he was doing. But I'm glad he has parents like you."

The breath left Tessa's lungs. "Oh…uh…we're not his parents. Luke has been helping me out at the foster group home that I run. I'm watching Tommy until they find a forever family for him."

Lily frowned. "But you guys are so good with him. And you love him—I can tell. Why don't you adopt him?"

Luke sighed, running his palm over the baby's head again. "It doesn't work that way."

"So strangers are going to get him? I'm not going to be able to see him?"

Tessa leaned forward, her gaze locking on Lily's. "I promise you that I will help you find a way to get back on your feet and stay in contact with whoever adopts Tommy. Open adoptions happen all the time."

Lily's eyes widened. "You mean I can like…see pictures of him growing up?"

Tessa grinned and nodded. "It's a definite possibility. Let me text Tommy's case manager and let her know what's going on."

While she was doing so, an older woman approached their table. Tessa blinked in surprise when she saw that it was Sylvia, one of the older ladies from the church. She was wearing an apron from the coffee shop.

"I'm sorry to interrupt your conversation, but I couldn't help overhearing. I think I can help."

Sylvia pulled out a chair and sat down at the table. "I own this coffee shop, and I'd like to offer this young woman a job."

Lily's mouth dropped open. "You would do that?"

The older woman nodded. "What do you want to do with your life? Do you have any plans?"

Lily shrugged. "I really didn't have a chance to think about it."

"Well, you have one now."

Tessa was thrilled with this turn of events. "Great! Now all we need is to find you a place to stay. I'm going to have Sierra run a background check on you and get you approved to stay with me at Harmony House."

Lily gasped. "You'd let me live with you?"

Tessa nodded. "As long as the state doesn't object, I would love the extra help around the house. And this way, you can be close to Tommy and an active part of helping decide where he's going to go for his permanent placement."

Lily was crying again, but this time it was happy tears. "I can't thank you enough for everything you're doing for me…and Tommy."

Tessa's heart was full. They had found a way to help her. "No problem at all. Now…do you want to hold your son?"

"Yes, please," the woman said enthusiastically. Luke handed over the baby, and Lily gushed over how good he looked and how much he had grown.

This time, it was Luke's and Tessa's eyes that were filled with happy tears as they witnessed the reunion of mother and son.

Chapter Fifteen

Sierra got back quickly to Tessa with the approval for Lily to move in with her. Luke volunteered to watch the kids at his house while Tessa took her to the shelter to pick up the few things she had.

"This is a cool house," Lily said when he entered his home. "I can't believe you gave it up for all these kids."

Luke just shrugged. "I had the space, and they needed it."

He was burping Tommy at the time, and Lily just stared at him like she was trying to figure him out.

"Were you really the one who was on the other side of the baby drop when I left him?"

Luke nodded. "Yeah, it was my night to watch the station. He was pretty crabby with everyone else except me. So I got to go to the hospital with him."

Lily reached out and touched one of Tommy's hands. "He must have been so scared."

"He wasn't alone for long. He had a whole crew of fire-fighters ready to spoil him. He still does. Plus, now he has about a dozen sets of grandparents too."

She smiled. "I'm glad he's going to have a big group of people that care about him."

Tessa put an arm around Lily. "You're part of that group now, too, Lily. You can stay as involved in his life as you want to be."

Lily bit her lip. "But what if his future parents don't want me to be?"

Tessa waved a hand. "If an open adoption is what you want, his case worker, Sierra, can make it happen. She's like a miracle worker. She might even let you interview some of the prospective parents to see who might be a good fit."

Lily's eyes were wide, like this could be too much information. "What if they are mean to me, for giving up the baby?"

Luke scowled. "They are going to have to say that to me as well. I'll sit with you and make sure nobody says anything they will later regret."

She gave him a big smile, then laughed when Tommy let out a big burp on Luke's shoulder.

"You're really good with him. I hope Tommy ends up with a father like you," Lily said.

Luke sighed. He wished that maybe the baby could have ended up with him as a father, but it wasn't meant to be.

"And you're wonderful with him too," Lily said, turning to Tessa. "I wish someone like you could be his mom."

Tessa's cheeks felt like they were on fire. She changed the conversation by showing Lily the cot she had set up for her in one of the rooms upstairs. "I know it's not much, but there will be a room for you once we get back to Harmony House."

Lily just smiled at her. "This is perfect."

Tessa left the younger woman to get settled and went down to talk to Luke. He was packing up his toolbox and getting ready to head over to do some construction work.

"It's been a long day already. I can't believe you're going to go do some more."

He shrugged. "It has to get done. We're on a timeline."

Tessa worried that he was pushing himself too hard for them. "Just…make sure you take some time to get plenty of rest."

Half of his mouth quirked up. "That's my line."

They shared a laugh.

Tessa watched him lean down and give the baby a kiss on the forehead before grabbing his keys. The baby wiggled his arms up at the firefighter, clearly thrilled to see him. Those two belonged together.

"What Lily said about you being the perfect dad for little Tommy… I think you should still put your name on the list. You never know what can happen."

He shook his head. "Sierra said the outlook for me even having a chance didn't look good."

Tessa gave a huff in frustration. He had given up before he had even tried.

"Please promise me you'll think about it. I think if you document to the state that you have an amazing support system in place that could help you with Tommy, that just because you would be a single dad doesn't mean he wouldn't have a huge family," she said. "If I could get approved to be a foster mom to ten kids when I'm single…you should be able to be considered to adopt one baby."

He sat in thought, as if he was considering her words. "But fostering and adopting are two different things. I would be promising to be his dad for forever."

Tessa gave him a soft smile. "Just because I'm a foster mother doesn't mean I have fewer qualifications."

His face dropped. "Tess, I didn't mean you weren't amazing at what you do. I'm just…"

She waved away his apology. "Scared. This would be a major change for you and a dramatic shift in your life plans. But sometimes God's plans don't always align with ours."

He put his face in his hands, deep in thought. Her fingers itched to reach out and offer him comfort, but she let him process what she had said.

"Do you really think I can do this?"

He finally looked up from his hands, his eyes full of… hope?

Tessa nodded. "I do. And I think you would be amazing at it."

Luke put his hands up. "I will think about it. But, Tess…"

He stood from his chair and crossed to her, pulling her in for a hug. "Thank you for believing in me. You don't know how much it means."

She leaned into the hug. It was warm and welcoming. *I could stay here all day*, she thought with surprise.

"Of course I believe in you," she said. "Look how much you've done for me already. And we were strangers a week or so ago."

She would write a letter to the state herself if she had to. It was so important that he understood how much he had to offer the world. How much he had done for her.

"We're not strangers now," Luke said, his voice taking on a tenderness that had her looking up at him. Her face came up to just below his chin. She only had to stand up on her tiptoes and she could be at the perfect height to kiss him.

She didn't know where that strange thought came from, but he must have had similar ideas, because his eyes dropped to her lips and he slowly leaned downward. Tessa's heels started to rise, trying to close the distance.

A throat cleared from behind them, and they stepped apart.

"Um…hey…sorry for interrupting. I just stopped by to play with the grandkids a bit. I knocked, but I don't think either of you heard me."

Tessa's face felt like it was on fire when she saw Luke's father standing there. She wished the ground would open up and swallow her whole.

"Uh, yeah, no worries. Luke was just getting ready to head out to the house to get some work done."

The older man nodded. "Sounds good. What about you? Isn't this supposed to be your day off?"

They told him about Lily and that Tessa needed to be here the rest of the day to help her settle in.

"I really need to go. The guys are going to think I abandoned them," Luke said.

Thomas eyed his son, and Tessa bit her lip at the concern in his expression. "I'll walk you out."

She was suddenly alone in the kitchen. Tessa didn't know everything they were talking about, but she was sure the father and son would definitely talk about her…and the kiss she and Luke had almost shared.

"You were a frequent visitor at my house before, Dad, but I see you just about every day now," Luke said as they approached his truck. "I think that you are taking to this grandfather role very seriously."

His father shrugged. "What can I say, I love all those kids already. It's fun being a grandpa, even if it's only for a short amount of time."

Luke rolled his eyes. "You're already a grandpa. Or are you forgetting your daughter's children?"

His niece and nephew were adorable, and they loved to climb all over his dad whenever they would visit.

"Yes, well, the more the merrier," his dad said with a laugh. "You know, I never would have expected your house to be lively like this. It's always so calm and quiet here. But I have to say, I kind of like it now."

Luke grinned. "I do too."

His father's eyebrows shot up. "You do? I never thought you wanted a life like this."

He hadn't. But now…it felt…right. "It's growing on me."

The older man studied him for a minute. "Are we going to talk about what I almost walked in on?"

Luke felt his cheeks warm. He had almost kissed Tessa. It wasn't something he'd planned. They were just caught up in the moment.

"It shouldn't have happened. I'm glad you interrupted us," he said.

His dad leaned up against the door of the truck, effectively blocking Luke from leaving until they had this conversation.

"You like her."

Luke nodded. "Of course I do. We've become good friends."

That earned him a scowl. "You know what I mean. You have feelings for her."

This was the exact thing he was trying to avoid thinking about. It was too complicated, and made things too murky when it came to his life plan. Luke ran his fingers through his hair.

"Okay…she's beautiful. And kind. And yes… I may have

some…romantic feelings toward her." The admission came out in a ramble. It felt strange to put them into words. There was no taking them back now. "But we want two different things out of life. So even if we do feel a pull toward each other, nothing can come of it."

He wondered if Tessa was starting to have feelings toward him… Another thought he hadn't allowed himself to consider.

"I don't think that's true at all. I think once you sit down and think about it, you don't want different things in life at all," his father challenged.

"But my plans—"

The older man gave him a disappointed look that used to have him shaking in his boots as a kid. "Plans change. Don't be so stubborn."

And with that, his father stepped away from the truck, clapped him on his back and sent him on his way.

The conversation ran through his head repeatedly the whole way to Harmony House. What had his father meant by he and Tessa wanting the same things in life?

When he got to the house, a tour of all the work his crew had been doing was an excellent distraction from the emotions he didn't want to process. But they soon came rushing back when he saw all the work they had accomplished and he realized how close they were to being done.

Tessa and the kids would be moving back here soon. She had told him that Sierra was setting up interviews with prospective adoptive parents for Tommy. He wouldn't be needed around the house anymore. There would be less of a reason for him to be here during all his free time.

They were friends, but he wouldn't see her every day. An ache filled his chest at the idea of not having Tessa's smile to cheer him up every day. Of not singing Tommy to sleep every night. Or flipping pancakes with Zack every day.

He had caught feelings, all right… But were they enough to make him abandon his perfectly laid plans?

Chapter Sixteen

Though they still stayed at Luke's house at night, Tessa and the little ones spent their days leading up to the state inspection at Harmony House. They were putting all the finishing touches on getting the rooms ready, and the kids were running around, excited over all the changes that had been made.

However, there were some things that were hiding under sheets. Luke declared them a surprise to be revealed later. He had such excitement in his eyes when he talked about it, she didn't want to spoil his fun. He had done so much for her by taking on this project that he deserved to find joy in it wherever he could.

She was in the kitchen making lunch one afternoon when the door to the den opened and a disgruntled-looking couple came walking out.

"Have a nice day," she called out as they went out the front door, but they just scowled at her.

"I'm guessing that didn't go well," she said to Lily and Luke, who excited the den after them.

Since Lily was now involved in Tommy's life, Sierra had asked her to be part of the process of screening prospective adoptive parents. The young woman had immediately roped

Luke into the process, and the two of them had been veto-ing people all week. Sierra was beyond frustrated.

"Oh, come on, guys. What was wrong with them?" Sierra said from the front door, coming inside after walking the couple to the car.

Lily sniffed. "They already have like, four kids. They don't need another. He wouldn't get the attention he deserves."

Luke nodded in agreement, his arms crossed.

Tessa snorted. "You do realize that he currently lives in a home with nine other kids?"

Lily shrugged. "Yeah, well, it's different here. There are plenty of people around here that take care of him. There's only two of them."

Sierra scowled. "You two can't keep running people off. He needs to find a forever family."

The two of them had been quite resolute in their rejection of candidates. Tessa would laugh about it if she knew that wouldn't pour even more gasoline on the fire that was Sierra's anger.

Lily bit her lip and kicked at the floor. "I know… I'm sorry."

Sierra laid a hand on her arm. "Are you changing your mind? Do you want to keep Tommy?"

Lily's head shot up. "No! I mean, I love him…but…no. I'm still not ready to be his mother. We just have to find the right people."

The girl looked up and met Tessa's eyes, a pleading look in them, and then she turned her gaze to Luke with the same expression.

"I have to go check on the little kids," she murmured, rushing from the room.

Sierra turned to Luke, her eyes narrowed to slits. "Okay, so what's your excuse for scaring off everyone?"

Luke looked surprised. "I'm not scaring off anyone!"

Tessa laughed. "You're a six-four fireman who sits across the table and glares at people while Lily takes advantage of their weakness and asks very leading questions."

He shrugged. "I don't see a problem in that at all. We have to use everything in our arsenal to find him a good home."

Sierra opened her mouth to scold him more, but he was saved by a call from upstairs from one of his crew.

The case worker huffed and sat down at one of the counter seats. "This is becoming an impossible task. I thought finding a permanent placement for Tommy would be easy. I never should have given them veto power."

Tessa bit her lip to hide her smile. "Yeah, that's not the way the state usually does things."

Sierra threw up her hands in frustration. "This is what I get for being nice. I mean, our ultimate goal is reunification, but Lily has made it clear that she's not interested."

Tessa paused for a moment, considering her response.

"I…uh…think that Lily keeps vetoing people because she wants Luke to be Tommy's dad," she said.

The young woman wanted Tessa to be the boy's mom, too, but that wasn't happening, so she wouldn't mention it to the case worker.

Sierra frowned. "He asked me about it, but he never put his name on the list."

"Because you told him it was impossible for him to adopt when so many couples wanted him."

The other woman huffed. "I never said 'impossible.' I just said that it was more likely a couple would get picked.

But now that the birth mother is involved and she has a preference, it could be another point in his favor."

Tessa arched an eyebrow at that. "You didn't think to mention that to him?"

Sierra shook her head. "Again, I thought he wasn't really interested. That he was just asking hypothetical questions."

Sure, Luke had his life plans, which did not involve adopting a child before he got married, but Tessa had a feeling he would jump at the opportunity to be Tommy's father. "I think you should ask him."

Sierra smiled. "I think that he does have a chance. If I can convince the state that they should choose him over the other waiting couples."

"You would do that for him?"

She nodded. "He'd be an easier sell if he was married, but not an impossible one. Especially if you and Lily speak up for him."

Tessa's eyebrows shot up in surprise. "Me? Why do I have a say in this?"

"Because you've been his caregiver since he first came into foster care. You've been the one who has spent the most time with both him and Luke. A glowing letter from you would go a long way toward him getting approval."

Tessa was already drafting the letter in her head. "I will get it to you by the end of the day."

She was excited and couldn't wait to break the news to Luke that he still had a chance with Tommy.

"You know, I'm surprised that Lily isn't pushing for you to adopt him, based on how much that girl admires you," Sierra said.

Tessa and Lily had become close in the past week. She was teaching the girl to bake, and it was lovely to see her blossom without the stresses of life weighing her down. She was also thriving in her new job at the coffee shop, becoming more confident with each day.

"Uh, she has mentioned that she thinks I should be Tommy's mom," Tessa said shyly.

Sierra arched a brow. "Along with Luke being his dad?"

Tessa's cheeks heated as she nodded.

Her friend chuckled. "Well, I think I can speak for everyone who has spent time with you and Luke over the past few weeks when I say that we could see the two of you together."

Tessa opened her mouth to deny what Sierra was saying, but the other woman continued, "And I've been meaning to tell you… Harmony House has taken on a new life since he became involved in it. You were doing an amazing job on your own, but the two of you… It's been something special lately."

Tessa had to admit that the kids cherished the extra love and attention they got from Luke when he came over every day. Zack, especially, had thrived under his care.

"But I was doing fine on my own. I can do this," Tessa said, her old fear of looking weak rearing its ugly head.

Sierra came around and hugged her. "I know that it's been important to you to prove that you can do this on your own, and you have. But you and Luke…you've complemented each other here in a way that really creates an amazing environment for these kids."

Tessa backed away from her friend and leaned against the kitchen counter, considering her words. She and Luke had formed a sort of unit in the past several weeks. The thought of going back to life without him being a regular part of it was…unbearable.

And just his company alone, she had looked forward to talking to him every day. To have someone to share her life with, someone who cared for her. Still, she couldn't ask him to take on all this in the long-term.

"I don't think he could handle all the chaos my life mission would bring. There's a difference between adopting one baby and spending time with us for a couple of weeks, and a lifetime of fostering ten kids at once," she said.

Sierra laughed. "Need I remind you that he seems to be handling it all this time so far and we've seen no cracks in his resolve? You two have worked beautifully together in the past few weeks."

"But my mission has always been to do this alone."

Sierra gave her a tender smile. "Maybe it's time to open yourself up to the possibility that he's been the partner you've been waiting for. Maybe it's time for a new mission."

Tessa considered her friend's words. Was she too caught up in proving to herself that she could do this alone? Many people had told her that she needed to be open to help. And now that she had support, she loved it.

Between Luke's life plans and her mission—were the two of them closing themselves off to the possibility of something better?

Her thoughts were interrupted when Lily came bursting back into the kitchen. "I have the most amazing news!"

She shared that Sylvia had just called from the coffee shop—telling her that she was such a great addition to the shop that they wanted to hire her on full-time. "And…she said I can rent the apartment above the shop at a discounted rate! I'm going to have a home, all of my own!"

Tessa would be sad to see the girl go, but she knew what

a momentous thing this was for her. "That is wonderful news. I hope you won't be a stranger."

Lily threw herself into Tessa's arms. "I won't, I promise. I can't believe everyone is being so nice to me."

"You deserve it, sweetie," Tessa said.

Lily ran out to go find Luke to tell him the good news, and Tessa couldn't wipe the smile off her face. "You know, a few weeks ago, I said the same thing. I couldn't understand why people were being so nice to me."

Sierra chuckled. "Yeah, that church group has formed a habit of just adopting people who need them."

Tessa got back to work on lunch. "Maybe it's time that I went back to church."

Sierra tilted her head, studying her. "Why did you stop going in the first place? Didn't you say your foster mom took you?"

Tessa nodded. "Yeah, but I just had a hard time letting people into my life. You've seen from this group that sometimes church people involve themselves in your business and life whether you want them to be or not. I was never ready before."

"And you are now?"

Tessa laughed. "Ready or not—they're here."

"They sure are. And it doesn't look like you'll be getting rid of them anytime soon, not that you want to. Will it be difficult for you to go back to church?"

Tessa shook her head. "I don't think so. I never really lost my faith."

"Why not?"

"I always liked the reassurance that while I had a terrible father growing up, I had a better Heavenly Father. It was even more comforting after my parents were gone," Tessa explained.

Her friend slung an arm over her shoulder. "You were never alone. And now you have even more people to love you."

Tessa smiled, growing content with the knowledge that she never had to go back to handling everything by herself ever again. And though that had been her original mission, it was in the process of changing, for the better.

Chapter Seventeen

"Why am I covering my eyes?" Tessa complained. "I was literally in Harmony House two days ago."

Luke's deep chuckle sounded in her ear. "Well, you need to for the grand reveal. Besides, we added some last-minute details since you last saw it."

The kids were back at Luke's house with the volunteers, and he had been so excited when he picked her up this morning to drive her over to Harmony House that Tessa couldn't help but catch his contagious enthusiasm.

"Can I look now? Please?"

"Okay, Tess, check out your new and improved home."

She dropped her hands and gasped. It looked...beautiful. There was a large wooden sign in the yard—hand carved, from the looks of it—that said "Harmony House." Pots of mums lined the sidewalk, and there was a swing on the front porch.

"That's for all your serious conversations you have with the kids who need it," Luke pointed out.

Tessa gave a sigh of contentment. He really did understand the importance of this place. When they were here the other day, the furniture hadn't been moved back in. Some of it was too destroyed by the flood to save, but it had all been from the thrift store anyway. Luke had assured her that the church group was scouring the town for replacements.

What he did not tell her was that they had purchased entirely new furniture for the entire house. She gasped when she entered. Everything was so functional and organized, just like Luke liked it. There were cubbies for toys, and strings with laundry pins to hang photos.

But while it was organized, it still had the feel of Tessa and her little family's chaos. The place wasn't sterile. It was filled with textiles and colors. It was warm and cozy.

Organized chaos. She didn't know such a thing existed, but Luke had created it for her. Maybe they did complement each other.

"When did you have time to do all this? I know you guys were on shift the last two days!"

He grinned. "I switched with someone else so I could have the time off. It was too important. And honestly, once word got out about what we were doing, the entire community chipped in, both financially and through man power."

Her brows furrowed. "The entire community?"

Luke nodded. "Yeah, not just the church people. The whole town believes in what you're doing here and wants to be part of Harmony House's mission. It takes a village, right? Come on, let's go see the upstairs."

She followed him and gasped when she got to the top of the landing. This was the part of the house that had undergone the most change since everything had been ruined in the flood.

The ugly old carpet was now replaced with tiles that looked like hardwood. The rooms had all been repainted, and new beds had been built for each kid.

She had a supply closet that held extra cots, blankets,

toys, diapers and other kids' supplies she might need for an upcoming placement.

"The church group is going to restock that every few weeks," Luke said. "And they also started a collection of old suitcases. We didn't like the story about how they carry all their items in a garbage bag."

The bathroom had been completely gutted and redesigned, with shorter sinks and toilets for the little ones.

"And now, are you ready to see the best part of the upstairs?"

Tessa nodded, still dumbfounded by everything she was seeing. "What more could there be?"

"Your room," he said.

"What?"

She wasn't used to people in her personal space, but she had left all the remodel decisions up to Luke. And she trusted him.

"I hope you like it."

He was so excited that he was bouncing on his toes, waiting for her to open the door to her room.

When she did, she gasped at the sheer comfort of the place. The softest quilt was on her bed, with what looked like a dozen throw pillows. A curtain of fairy lights hung along the top of one of her walls. The lighting in the room was soft and warm, giving it a cozy feeling.

"This is where you're going to go to rest when you need a moment," Luke said.

Tessa was completely speechless at everything he has done for her. She didn't even know where to begin when it came to thanking him. From her window, she could see her van pull up in front of the house, with Thomas driving. Her kids jumped out and slammed the front door open, screaming at a decibel that was hard to understand what they were saying. They ran around the house, excited over all the changes.

"I guess they like it," Luke teased.

"Like it? They are obsessed," Tessa said.

"There is a LEGO table," called one voice from the new playroom.

"Look in the backyard! There is a swing set and a playhouse!"

Tessa heard an "oof" and looked over to see Luke wrapped in a big bear hug from Zack. "Thank you so much. This is awesome."

Each of the kids kept running up to Luke and giving him big bear hugs too.

Tessa felt tears running down her cheeks. For so long, she had been doing this all alone, but she didn't have to anymore. She didn't want to.

She had come to rely on Luke's presence in her life. He wasn't just helping with her life's mission, he had become an integral part of it.

"Why are you crying? Is there something you don't like?"

The concern in Luke's voice made her cry even harder. The kids, now worried by her tears as well, all started hugging her and trying to climb on her lap at once. She was so surrounded with love. Her heart was ready to burst.

She looked up at Luke, her tears still streaming down her face. "I cannot thank you enough. There is no one I would rather have helping me with these kids than you."

Luke's gaze locked on hers over the kids' heads. He had tears in his eyes too. And something clenched in her heart.

She loved him. The realization had her gasping. She was in love with Luke. But she had no idea what to do about it.

Tessa watched him pick up Tommy and snuggle the baby close. Those two really belonged together. She may not know what to do about her feelings for Luke, but she could help with something else important to him.

She went to her desk and pulled out her stationery, a plan for the rest of the day in place.

Luke called Sierra back on his way home. She had left him multiple messages throughout the day, but he had been too busy to talk.

He was grateful to have something to do on the drive home to fill the overwhelming silence that hit him once he'd pulled away from Harmony House.

"You said you had something to tell me about Tommy? Did you find a family for him? I don't remember meeting anyone who fit the bill," he said.

Sierra laughed. "Well, in a way, we did find a place for him. And I think he might be someone you approve of."

Luke doubted it. No one seemed good enough for his favorite little guy. "Did Lily approve?"

"As a matter of fact, she did. She sent a letter of recommendation to my email this morning," Sierra said.

Lily hadn't said anything to him today about finding a family for Tommy. He couldn't help but feel a little hurt that he wasn't included in the process.

"Oh, well, I hope they give him a good life," Luke said, his voice catching. It was going to be so hard to let that little guy go.

Sierra chuckled. "I'm sure you will."

Luke gripped the steering wheel tighter. "Wait, what?"

Was she saying what he thought she was saying? "What are you talking about, Sierra?"

She cleared her throat. "I know you were only asking me hypothetically a while ago, but I'm going to recommend you as the adoptive parent for Tommy, if you're really interested."

He couldn't believe his ears. "Why this sudden turnaround?"

Sierra reminded him that he was the only person who could calm Tommy down when he was upset. And that he had been with him since the moment the baby was left in the safe-baby drop.

"And there's the fact that I received a very compelling document from Tessa this morning, outlining all the ways that you are perfect to be a successful parent to him. And a list containing all the people that are included in your support system. It's very long," Sierra said.

Tessa had sent that information about him? That must have been what she was preoccupied with all day. It had seemed like she had time to talk to everyone but him.

"That's… I don't know what to say."

Sierra continued, "There are also letters of recommendation from your father, the other firefighters at your station and members of your church. Tessa gathered them all today for you."

Luke was speechless. Tessa hadn't said anything to him. He couldn't believe she had done that.

"Luke, are you still with me? Do you still want this baby?"

Moment of truth. This was not in his perfect life plan. But if the past month had taught him anything, it was that the best things in life were what he hadn't expected. He needed to be open for God's surprise blessings.

And that included becoming a parent to Tommy. "I'm in," he said. The moment he said the words, they felt right.

"Great! I just have to wait for the final approval from the state, and then we can start the process."

He was doing this. It was happening. Luke was going to be a dad. And there was one person he wanted to share his joy with.

Maybe, if he was opening himself to changes in his life plan, that should include his feelings for Tessa.

Chapter Eighteen

The day of the state inspection had finally arrived. Tessa paced the house with a nervous energy all morning. The big kids were off at school. The little ones were at the church with the volunteers. She was all alone with her anxiety. Well, not alone.

She said a quick prayer and decided to stop pacing and sit at the table and wait instead. Tessa jumped out of her seat within a minute, however, because the doorbell rang. Were they early? They weren't expected for another twenty minutes.

Tessa took the time to straighten her outfit before opening the door. Instead of the inspectors or Sierra, it was Luke standing there.

"What are you doing here? I thought you had to work today."

He shrugged. "I switched shifts so I would have the day off. Did you think I was going to miss this?"

"You did all that so you could be here with me?"

Luke nodded. "It's going to be a stressful day. I figured you would need someone by your side."

Tessa's breath caught in her throat. "Thank you."

He opened his mouth to reply, but Sierra's voice sounded behind them.

"Hello? Anyone home? Well of course you're home, you have an inspection in like twenty minutes," Sierra said, poking her head in the door. "Oh, hey, guys! Thought I would come early to give some moral support before I had to be all official."

Tessa laughed. "Well, thank you. I can use all the support I can get."

They did a walk-through of the house, making sure everything was in order before the inspection. She still couldn't get over how much Luke and his crew had done to the place. It not only looked like a home, but a functioning foster center for a wide range of children's ages. It was what she had always dreamed of.

The doorbell rang. Her stomach flipped. This was it.

Luke threaded his fingers through hers. "You've got this. It's going to be great. You've built a beautiful thing here."

Sierra gave her a pointed look, glancing down at their joined hands and then back up to her face. "Yes, you really have."

Tessa felt her cheeks heat. She loosened her grip on Luke, but he held her hand firmly. He nodded at the door. "Let's do this."

She opened it, welcoming the group into her home. There were four of them. One was an older man who had a big grin on his face. He immediately set Tessa at ease. He introduced himself as Mr. Carter. Next to him was a lady who looked far less pleased to be there. She had a clipboard in her hand and a stern look on her face. She was Mrs. Saint-John. She was followed by a woman in her midforties, who greeted them with a smile and introduced herself as Mrs. Miller. She bore an overworked and underpaid air, much like all the other case managers whom Tessa had met. Finally, a younger man, named Mr. Runyon, came in with a tablet in his hands, ready to take down notes.

Tessa tried to calm her nerves, but speaking in front of an audience was not her forte. She welcomed the group to her home, then took them room from room, rotating between explaining their function and talking about the mission of the place.

Mr. Runyon checked every single medicine cabinet and the cabinets under the sink. Tess was glad they asked Luke and his crew to lock everywhere there might be cleaning supplies or medicine.

The group seemed impressed with the well-designed bedrooms and the increase in capacity from the bunk beds Luke had included in the redesign.

Tessa shared some of the success stories of the kids who had come through her door. Some had been reunited with their parents. Some had moved on to other foster homes or adoption. But all of them had a safe and happy place to stay while they waited for what came next. They were cared for and loved.

As Tessa guided the tour of Harmony House, she couldn't help but feel hope for all the future children it would bless. She said a quick prayer that her home would be approved and kids would continue to be placed here for years to come. The group didn't ask any questions as they toured the house, and she didn't know if that was a good or bad thing. Luke held her hand throughout the entire presentation. His calm presence giving her the courage she needed to get her message across.

"How do you have time to take care of so many children,

to make sure they have one-on-one time with a grown-up?" Mrs. Miller asked.

"It's simple—we use so many volunteers. I've learned the beauty of that this month too. I don't know if Sierra told you, but I grew up in the foster system."

The group leveled her with sympathetic gazes.

"My whole adult life, it has been very difficult for me to learn to ask for and accept help. I'm used to being alone, so it's hard to let go of that. Harmony House has helped me grow in that capacity too. There are so many people from several different generations who help out. People are making connections and getting to know each other. And you can't imagine what a great support system these kids will have by growing up in this town."

They finished the tour in the dining room, at the table filled with snacks she and the kids had made yesterday. The kids had each made a craft project for the inspectors too. She was hoping it softened their hearts a little bit.

"Nice touch," Luke whispered under his breath.

"Thought it couldn't hurt," she replied.

While everyone was enjoying their snacks, Tessa asked if they had any questions.

Mr. Carter shook his head. "You did a very thorough job in your presentation. I've been with the department for thirty-seven years, and I can honestly say I've never seen anything like this."

Tessa winced. "In a good way or a bad way?"

The older man laughed. "Definitely in a good way. This is nothing short of phenomenal. The impact you are making in those kids' lives and the community you've built with all the people helping with this place…it's wonderful."

The rest of the group nodded, even the lady with the

stern look on her face. "We will definitely be looking to reproduce what you've done here throughout the state. We hope you will help us do that."

Tessa's jaw dropped. "Really? So I passed the inspection?"

Sierra laughed. "Passed? Of course you did. And I think they are offering you a job. Not only do they want you to continue this place, but they are going to pay you to help train others to open their own."

No more working nights on the telephone for her. This was a dream come true. Luke was looking down at her, pride beaming in his eyes.

"You did it," he said.

But she couldn't have done this without him. "We did it."

The inspectors continued to praise the Harmony House project, promising they would be in touch with her soon to talk plans for expansion. Sierra escorted them out, giving Tessa and Luke big hugs before leaving.

Once they were alone in the house, Tessa and Luke turned to each other and screamed in excitement. They held hands and jumped up and down.

"I can't believe that just happened," she said.

"I can. This place is amazing. You're amazing," Luke said.

She stopped jumping but kept hold of Luke's hands. "I know I've said 'thank you' like a million times. But this is all possible because of you."

He shook his head. "You would have found a way without me."

"No way!"

He reached out and tucked a strand of hair behind her ear. "I think I've created a monster. Now you are so used to letting people help you that you don't take any credit for yourself."

Tessa didn't know what came over her…she just wanted to show Luke just how much he meant to her. She stood up on her tiptoes and pressed her lips to his.

He froze.

She was mortified, and started to pull away, but Luke suddenly kissed her back.

They were interrupted by the sound of the kids coming home from school. They pulled apart abruptly.

"Did we make it? Did we pass?" Zack asked as he ran into the room.

"We did!" both Luke and Tessa shouted at the same time. They recreated the jumping-and-screaming scene from earlier, but with all the kids this time.

Once the celebration stopped, the kids dove into the leftover treats on the table.

"I'm sorry about that. There is never a moment of peace around here," Tessa said. She didn't know if she should bring up the kiss. She had barely any time to process what happened herself.

Luke grinned as he watched the chaos. "I was going to suggest taking you out to dinner to celebrate our victory, but a dinner here with the gang will be great as well."

Butterflies took flight in her stomach at the thought of him taking her out to dinner. They had been out to a meal together before, but now, after that kiss, it would probably be a date.

But was that what Luke wanted? Or had it just been a spur-of-the-moment thing on his part? All throughout dinner, while everyone around her chattered excitedly about the day, Tessa thought about their kiss. She was confused by it. They both agreed they wanted different things in life. Despite her feelings for him, she knew that fostering ten kids was not in his life plan.

But his actions were telling her something different. Was he enjoying this life after all?

Luke helped her tuck each of the kids in that night. They were thrilled by the new beds in their rooms and were hard to settle down. But he was a great storyteller, and soon they were all dozing.

Her next task was to clean up the playroom, which looked like a tornado had gone through it. Luke went to help her, but she protested. "You've already done so much today. Why don't you go home and rest?"

As per usual, he ignored that request and kept cleaning. Tessa waited for him to bring up the kiss but he remained silent on the subject.

And she definitely wasn't going to be the one to bring it up. She guessed he must be thinking it was a mistake.

"I can't believe how easily they turned this practically new room into a disaster area in a matter of hours," Luke said as he scooped up LEGO bricks into a bin. "It's going to take weeks to get my house back to normal after their stay."

Tessa's heart sank. That settled it for her. No matter how much she cared for Luke, he couldn't have this many kids in his life at a time. He couldn't handle the mess and chaos they brought.

No one could but her. She was better off alone. At least she had that kiss they'd shared as a lovely memory of what could have been.

Chapter Nineteen

Tessa was quiet the rest of the evening, and Luke couldn't help but wonder if she was regretting the kiss they'd shared. She barely looked at him. The evening was wearing thin, but he didn't want to leave. He came up with every excuse to hang out with the kids and to help with the chores, but once story time and tucking the little ones in was over—it was time for him to go.

"Oh, I almost forgot in the middle of all this excitement—thank you for all the stuff you sent to Sierra on my behalf about me adopting Tommy," he said. "I couldn't believe you did all that behind my back."

Tessa's cheeks turned pink. "I know you were still on the fence as to whether to put your name in or not. But the way you and Lily kept rejecting candidates…and every time I saw you with him… I just wanted to make sure that if you decided you wanted to try to adopt him that you would have everyone in your corner."

Luke grinned. "And by that, you mean literally every-one. Did you run around town all day handing out stationery to people?"

Tessa giggled. "It kind of felt like that."

"Well, thank you. Seriously. That's the nicest thing any-one's ever done for me," he said.

Tessa frowned. "Then you don't have enough nice people in your life, which doesn't seem true, since all the people who have helped me lately were brought in by you."

He rolled his eyes. "I'm thanking you. You could just say 'you're welcome.'"

"You're welcome. Seriously, though, I think you should adopt him. You would be an amazing father. I think every single kid in this place would agree."

Luke's heart swelled at her compliment. He had always wanted to be a dad, and it seemed he wasn't going to have to wait until the perfect circumstances to be one. "I decided to put my name on the list, and Sierra already chose me. She just needs final sign-off by the state, and then Tommy will be my son."

Tessa's eyes filled with happy tears as she threw her arms around him. "Oh, Luke, that's amazing news! I'm so happy for you! For both of you."

He pulled out of the hug and smiled down at her. "Well, like you said about me when it came to passing the inspection—I wouldn't have been able to do this without your help."

She shrugged. "I guess we're even now."

He tilted her chin up to meet her eyes. "Tess, friendship is reciprocal. There is no owed favors or breaking even. We just help each other whenever it's needed."

Tessa nodded, her eyes wide and glued to his. But then they blinked back into focus and she stepped away from him. And something flashed across her eyes. It looked a lit-tle like hurt, but it was gone too quickly for him to analyze.

"Yes, we have become really good friends throughout all

of this. Which is why it's going to be sad when you're not spending as much time around here as before," Tessa said.

He frowned. "What do you mean?"

She shrugged. "Well, Tommy won't be here much longer, so you won't need to come see him here anymore. The house is all fixed and we have more volunteers than ever before because of the church. So you really don't have the need to come here every day."

Luke's heart pounded in his chest. Was he kicking him out of her life? "Yeah, well, I thought we became close through all of this. I'm not just going to stop coming here because the remodel is over and Tommy is gone. I'll be here to see you and the other kids."

It dawned on him that she might be shutting him down because she had never had someone stick around in her life before. It made him regret their kiss all the more. While he would savor the memory of it forever, it had spooked her and it meant she was pushing him away. He would take Tessa in his life however he could have her—even as just a friend. Although he wished for more. It was clear that was too much to ask for her at this time.

"We're friends, right? We're still going to hang out from time to time?" he asked.

That sounded way too little for him, but he would start small until he found more excuses to be here.

"Of course we're friends. But you're in the search for a perfect woman to fit into your lifestyle and perfectly organized life. You and I both know I'm not that woman. I come with too much chaos. And spending a lot of time with me, even as a friend, will only get in the way of you finding the woman you need," Tessa said.

His heart shattered at her words. He was starting to

think that they could overcome their differences of life-styles, but it seemed she didn't even want to try. "But what about that kiss?"

It had solidified for him that Tessa was who he was meant to be with, and it broke his heart that she didn't feel the same.

"I think we both know it was a mistake. This is for the best, Luke," Tessa said.

She opened the front door. He still didn't want to go, but he had to respect her wishes.

"I'm going to be on shift for the next three days. Just… don't forget about me."

Her lips turned up at that. "As if I ever could."

"We'll talk about this more when I'm done and can come back."

She nodded, leaning up and giving him another hug. "Goodbye, Luke, thank you for everything."

It didn't just feel like a farewell for now, it felt more per-manent. In one short day, he had kissed the most beautiful and kind woman in the world. And he had also lost her.

When he got home, Luke realized how quiet and lonely his house was. He cleaned up some of the toys, but much of their clutter, he left around his home. That made it feel less empty in here.

Day one, getting ready for work, he missed the chaos of kids dancing to their morning cartoons and spilling milk in their kitchen.

Day two, he ran home on his lunch break, and there weren't any of those dinosaur nuggets he liked to grab off their plates.

Day three, when his shift was over, he missed walking into his house and receiving a beaming smile from Tessa.

He missed his family. He craved the chaos they brought into his house. He missed Tessa.

Finally, on day four, he was distracted by a phone call from Sierra. "I have some good news and some bad news for you."

He winced, hoping that the bad news wasn't too devastating. "Okay, go ahead."

"Well, the good news is that the state board loved your application and think you are a good candidate for adoption," Sierra said.

Luke's heart soared. Tommy was going to get to come home soon. His thoughts raced through all the things he had to do to get ready. He needed to go to the store and get a crib and all the other baby supplies he could think of.

Luke's mental checklist-making paused when he remembered something else: there was bad news. "Okay…and what's wrong?"

Sierra cleared her throat and said, "Well, through their case worker, another couple on the list for Tommy heard that you were the front runner. And they say that it wasn't fair that you were screening candidates. They are accusing you of sabotaging their interview so you could adopt the baby."

"What? That's ridiculous. I would never do that to anyone."

Sierra sighed at the other end of the phone. "I know that and you know that, but the board wants to meet with you in person."

"Okay."

"Tomorrow."

Luke cringed at that. He had taken a lot of time off since

the baby had first arrived in the drop box. "Okay, I will call my chief and ask if I can have the day off."

"I'm so sorry you have to do this. I think you're perfect for Tommy, but you know how some people can be."

Luke agreed. "Yes, well, if it's meant to be, everything will work out and I can adopt Tommy."

He went upstairs to the nursery, wondering if he should get started on redecorating Tommy's room. But was it too soon to assume the boy was going to come home?

What would Tessa do in this situation? he asked himself. She would probably not have this problem in the first place, he thought. She would have proved a long time ago that she was more than capable of caring for a baby.

All he could hope for the following day that it would end with little Tommy finding the very best forever home, whether that was with Luke or not.

Before she had ten kids, Tessa never ran late a day in her life. Nowadays, it was a frequent occurrence. She pulled into the state agency's parking lot, jumping out of the car almost the moment she reached a complete stop.

"Excuse me. I'm looking for the interview with Luke Russell and the adoption board? I need to give them some letters from the community."

The woman behind the reception desk arched an eyebrow. "From what I understand, this is just an informal conversation. They are not listening to testimony or anything."

Tessa's shoulders sagged. She wanted to help Luke be chosen for Tommy, but she didn't know how. "Can I at least go in there and watch?"

"You want to watch a conversation?"

Tessa nodded. "I care about the man and the baby involved. I'm his current foster mother, which means I'm invited to all hearings in this case."

Finally, she was waved to an office on the third floor. "You won't miss it," the receptionist said.

Tessa hurried up the stairs, hoping she would be there on time. Sure, this wasn't a trial or official hearing or anything, but she wanted to try to give testimony if they would let her. She made it up to the third floor and found Luke sitting alone in a long hallway. He was wringing his hands.

She sat down in the chair next to him, putting her hand over his. His head shot up.

"Tess? What are you doing here?"

Tessa frowned at him. "You were with me the whole time I was going through our foster care inspection, so I won't leave you to go through this alone."

He squeezed her hand. "Thank you so much. Lily is in there right now, explaining that she asked me to weigh in on the potential parents with her."

Tessa nodded. "I understand that this family really wanted to have a baby, but I can't believe they filed a complaint about you. It's just not fair. You don't deserve this."

Luke shrugged. "I get why they are doing it. I mean, perhaps I did veto a lot of good people because I didn't think anyone was good enough for Tommy. Maybe it was my subconscious doing it because I wanted him to be my kid."

"To be honest, I don't really think it matters. You have a lot of other things working in your favor besides just the parent interviews. You have a personal connection with the baby already. You already have your home approved by the state because we did an inspection. You have a stable job, you have the background clearance."

Footsteps sounded on the hard hallway floor, and Tessa

looked up, grinning. "And you have more than that… Look."

Sierra and about two dozen people were walking toward them. Luke stood up, his mouth dropping open. "What are all of you doing here?"

"We are going to talk to the state board one by one and tell them how much you deserve to be Tommy's dad."

He met Tessa's eyes. "You did this?"

She nodded. "Kind of. When I told some of them what was happening and that I was coming down here, they spread the news. We all believe in you, Luke. And we believe Tommy belongs to our family."

Luke's eyes roamed over the group. "I can't thank all of you enough for this. I didn't even know a month ago that I wanted to be a father, but now…it means the world to me."

The door to the room opened and Lily stepped out. Her eyes widened when she took in the group, and then she beamed. She turned to the people in the room behind her. "See, I told you. He's the best one. Look at all these people who want to talk to you."

Tessa recognized some of the people who had done her home inspection who were also on the board. They smiled proudly at the group. "Yes, I think we had better talk to Mr. Russell now and get to the bottom of things before this gets turned into a very long afternoon. We have read all the letters in your file," one of the women said. "I'm guessing that most of this testimony will be the same."

The group were talking all at once, shouting their support for Luke. Tessa had to cover her mouth to hold in her laugh.

"Okay, okay!" another man on the board said. "Let us

talk to Mr. Russell, and we will let you know if we need to hear more."

Luke gave the group a thumbs-up and a smile as he followed the board into the room. Before the door was closed, however, he reached out and grabbed Tessa's hand, pulling her in with him.

"Mr. Russell, this is just a conversation with you."

He shook his head. "She's part of my support system. I need her."

Tessa's stomach fluttered at his words. She promised not to speak in the meeting unless they asked her a question. She just sat next to Luke the entire time, holding his hand for moral support. They asked him only a few questions about the interview process he went through with Lily for the prospective parents, and about the timeline in his decision to adopt.

But that was it.

"Mr. Russell, the birth mother told us that she asked you for her support during the parent interviews. We spoke to the case manager, who had nothing but high praise for you. And her placement report on your home was remarkable. We have no doubt in our mind that you will be the very best father for Tommy."

The board broke out in applause, and Tessa's tears started flowing.

"What does that mean?" Luke asked.

"It means that you're officially Tommy's father. I think there will be more paperwork and an official hearing before the judge, but they've chosen you."

She gave him a huge hug, and soon the whole room was

filled with their friends and family, spreading their con-
gratulations. Tommy may not be related to them by blood,
but he was going to be part of a wonderful family.

Chapter Twenty

Luke was making list after list. Plan after plan. While his life plan had gone out the window, there was still the need to keep his daily life organized. Especially since there was so much to do. Right now he was making a list of all the supplies he needed to set up a room for Tommy.

Tessa had agreed to help him shop today, since it was Thursday and her day off from Harmony House. He was proud of her for accepting the regular babysitters and taking time for herself. He hadn't wanted her to spend her free time helping him, but she had insisted.

It wasn't the thrift shop this time. They drove two towns over to the department store with the cutest baby supplies, according to Tessa.

"Is this going to be another to cart trip?" he teased.

Tessa snorted. "You have absolutely no idea just how much stuff a baby needs. This might be a three- or four-cart trip."

She was right.

They picked out a crib, a rocking chair, blankets, toys, clothes—everything the little boy would need to get a fresh start in life. Another cart was filled with diapers, wipes, bottles, formula, bath supplies and more.

Luke really did have no idea what a baby needed. "How am I going to do this? I'm not a baby expert."

She laughed. "No first-time parent is. You kind of learn as you go. And you make mistakes. Lots of them. You learn from them. And then you make different mistakes."

And suddenly, he was terrified of this whole parenting thing. Tessa took pity on him and loaded a few baby guides in the cart as well. "You have a whole community of people behind you, some of whom have lots of experience. We won't let you fail," she said.

Luke was so thankful that Tessa was spending her day off with him. Those few days he had spent without her had been like torture. It had been far too long. He had almost dialed her phone number about a dozen times, but he didn't want to seem too needy.

However, the empty house had felt eerily quiet without her and the kids. The somber mood he was in whenever at home had only confirmed his suspicion that he now needed the chaos that she brought into his life. His life plan was already thrown out the window with the addition of Tommy to his family. And he knew that Tessa would make it even better.

He was in love with her. He just had to find a way to tell her. And to ask if she wanted to be Tommy's parent too.

When they entered Luke's house, Tessa blinked in surprise when she saw the mess that was still there from her time here with the kids.

"It looks so different from the first time I came over," she said. "You can still tell that kids lived here for a while. I thought you'd have everything back in order in no time."

Luke shrugged. "I kind of miss them. It feels more like

a home here now rather than just a house that's waiting for something to happen. It feels more lived in."

Tessa grinned at him. "Yeah, my house feels like it's lived in by a whole group of tornadoes."

He laughed. "The very best tornadoes. They're welcome to come over here anytime they want. You too. You especially."

"Maybe I'll come visit you every Thursday when I have time off," she said.

"I like the sound of that."

But he didn't want a whole week to go by without seeing Tessa. It didn't feel right.

He kept silent on the subject, though, while they got the bedroom set up for Tommy. They chatted away, talking about their week and their time apart. Tessa seemed to be getting the hang of things without Luke there every day. He wished didn't have to.

"You're not going to believe this," Luke said.

She paused in her onesie-folding project to look up at him.

"What?"

"All the instructions for building the crib are in another language. I have no idea how to put this together," Luke said.

Tessa laughed. "Well, it's your lucky day because I've assembled and disassembled so many cribs in my life time."

He watched in amazement as she put the crib together in thirty minutes, flat. "I'm starting to believe that you are talented at everything."

She grinned. "Only completely random things that seem to not be very important."

Once the room looked fit for its future occupant, Tessa

started getting ready to go home. *It's now or never*, Luke told himself.

"I really should get going and relieve the babysitter," she said.

Luke shook his head. "I asked them if they could stay a little later than usual tonight."

Her eyes rounded in surprise. "You did? Why?"

"I want to take you out to dinner. It's the least I can do for how you showed up for me at the courthouse the other day."

Tessa frowned. "We show up for each other. It's what we do. Besides, a wise man once told me that doing things for a friend wasn't reciprocal."

He was starting to hate the word *friend* because he wanted so much more than friendship with Tessa. Sure, she had become his best friend over the past month, but he wanted her to be more than that.

"Please just come to dinner with me. I've missed spending time with you."

Her cheeks turned a lovely shade of pink.

"I've missed spending time with you too. All right, one dinner," Tessa said. "We can't stay out too late, and we have to stop and get a dessert to bring home to the kids."

He grinned. "It's a deal."

"So, where are you taking me—to a fancy meal? Fast food?" Tessa asked as he drove through town.

"Nope, it's a surprise," he said, looking as excited as a schoolboy. Something had changed between them since the custody meeting for Tommy. They were dancing around something, but Tessa wasn't going to be the first one to bring it up. She had been the one to kiss him in the first place and then he hadn't wanted to talk about it after that.

Now the ball was in his court. If Luke ever wanted anything more between them, it would be up to him to make the first move.

She gasped when he pulled into a mountainside park that had a little pull-off area and a picnic table. It had the most gorgeous view she had ever seen in her entire life. Tessa had lived in this mountain town for a long time but hadn't taken time to explore much of the beautiful vistas that they had in the area. She had been too focused on Harmony House to really see the beauty of the world around her.

"We're eating here?"

Luke hopped out of his truck and ran around to open the door for her. Once she was out of the vehicle, he reached into the back of his truck to grab something. "Yep, I packed us a picnic today. The warmer days are coming along fewer and far between, so I wanted to enjoy the outdoors with you before fall fully sets in."

Her brow furrowed in confusion. "But you didn't know I would go to dinner with you. It was kind of a last-minute decision."

He laughed. "I was hoping you'd say yes. I had this plan in the works since before breakfast this morning. That's when I packed the basket."

She rolled her eyes "You're pretty confident in yourself."

"I was just hopeful. Not confident."

She swiped at his arm. "As if I'd say no."

Tessa watched in awe as he unpacked a meal of sandwiches, her favorite chips, carrots and hummus, and a strawberry cheesecake. All her favorites were there. He'd even brought her a bottle of the strawberry lemonade she always grabbed whenever she stopped for refreshments while they were out and about.

"You thought of everything. When did you have time to do all this?"

He smiled. "Well, my house has been a little more boring lately for some reason. I seem to have a lot more spare time on my hands. Especially since I'm not remodeling a whole house anymore."

She laughed. "Whatever are you going to do with yourself?"

Luke leaned forward and booped her nose. "I'm sure you will be able to come up with a list of things for me to do every week. I'm not giving up on helping at Harmony House," he said. "Even if you insist that you don't need me anymore."

Tessa gasped. "I never said that! I just meant you didn't have to help out if you have better things to do."

He frowned at her. "There are no better things to do than that. I want to be there for everything. For the good days when it's just all about making pancakes and playing catch. And the bad days when something breaks and there is a food fight and you need all hands on deck. I'm going to be there for both."

Tessa's breath caught in her throat at his speech. "But what about your plan? Aren't you going to try to find your perfect wife so you can have your perfect family?"

Luke reached out and cupped her cheek. "Tess, I had a vision of how I thought my life should go. I wanted everything to fit perfectly and go according to plan. I wanted to keep everything regimented because I got scared when I had no idea what to expect. But the more I tried to hold on to that plan, the more God threw things into my life to shake me up."

Tessa thought about all the things that had happened to the both of them in the past month. Nothing had gone as expected, but yet it had turned out for the better.

Luke continued, "It's been quite the reminder that my plans mean nothing. And God's the only one with the perfect plan. And He already sent me the perfect woman."

Tessa gasped, but he leaned down and stopped it with a sweet kiss.

"You're the woman I love and the one I want to make organized chaos with for the rest of my life," Luke said.

Tessa blinked back tears. She couldn't believe he felt the same way about her. It seemed too good to be true. Could she trust that he really wanted to be part of her life, including the mission she had pledged herself to?

"Are you sure you can handle all my kids? All the mess and spontaneity they bring? Ten kids at any given time is a lot."

He grinned. "These past few weeks have been the happiest of my life. The days when I wasn't there were the loneliest and saddest. I'm part of your mission now. I'm in for life, if you'll have me."

Tessa nodded. "I'll have you. I love you, too, Luke. So much."

Luke arched a brow at that. "Are you sure? I thought you wanted to only be friends with me and also prove that you could do everything in Harmony House on your own."

She wrapped her arms around his waist. "I think that my mission is much better with the right kind of person by my side."

After her parents died, Tessa had been all alone in the

world. She went from home to home. Forming attachments had been difficult, so finding someone she wanted to let into her life felt like a miracle. She had gone from being all alone a month ago to being part of a community and being loved by Luke.

"But there's one more thing," Luke said, looking nervous. "I…um…am kind of a package deal now. I'm going to be a father, so being in a relationship with me means there is a high likelihood that you will someday be…"

"Tommy's mother," she said, and he nodded.

It was only fitting, considering they met the night the little boy entered both their worlds. If only they had known then what an impact he would make on their lives. "Well, Lily will be happy. She wanted us to each be his parent."

Luke grinned and pulled her into his arms. They stood watching the sun set over the mountains.

"Tessa, I have to ask you something."

Her heart rate sped up. Was he asking what she think he might be asking? Was it too soon?

"Y-yes?" she replied, her voice barely coming out as a squeak.

"Will you go out with me on your day off next Thursday?"

"Oh," she said, trying to hide the disappointment in her voice. "Sure."

"And every Thursday for the rest of our lives?"

She grinned up at him. "Sounds like a perfect plan to me."

They sealed their agreement on their new life plan with a kiss.

Epilogue

Six months later...

The sun was shining brightly on the day of Tessa and Luke's wedding. It took place at the church they both attended. It was packed to the brim with church members, firefighters, foster kids and other community members who supported them.

Even though it had been six months since they first got together, it felt to Tessa like this day had been a long time coming.

"Absolutely stunning, my dear," Sylvia said, helping Tessa adjust her gown. "I'm so glad we picked this one."

She looked down at the beautiful gown she was wearing. It looked very similar to the wedding dress she had seen on her mother in one of the few family pictures she had managed to save from her childhood. Sylvia and the other church ladies had taken her dress shopping. They had been really into it, cheering or booing dresses as she tried them on. She almost felt like her mother was there with her.

Sylvia had basically been her stand-in mother for this entire planning process. Lily was learning to become a baker, and the older woman sent her away to a cake-decorating class so she could make their wedding cake. She was proudly dressing like the mother of the bride today and telling everyone how proud she was of her beautiful Tessa.

Tessa didn't have a lot of friends in her life, so it went without saying that Sierra was her maid of honor.

"Why do you have worry frowns?" Sierra said as they prepared for their trek down the aisle.

"Only you would point out a bride's beauty flaws," Tessa teased.

"Oh, you're beautiful, don't get me wrong," she said. "But something's bothering you. Come on, out with it."

Tessa bit her lip.

"What if I'm bad at it?"

"Bad at what?"

"Being part of a family. Being a wife. Maybe the reason I moved around foster homes so much is that something is wrong with me and they didn't want me," Tessa said.

Sierra gave a heavy sigh. "Honey, that man up there loves you. You can practically see the cartoon hearts his eyes turn into whenever he looks at you."

Tessa looked at Luke the same way. "Do you think I can be someone with a family?"

Sierra nodded. "You're not broken. The system didn't break you—it made you stronger."

They hugged before it was Sierra's turn to walk down the aisle.

Luke's dad would be the one giving her away today. The man had shed a few tears when she asked him. The rest of the pickleball club didn't speak to her for a week because they thought they all should have been picked instead.

"You look so pretty," Lily whispered from her side as

they watched the bridesmaids saunter down the aisle. "That dress is amazing."

She was holding their ring bearer, Tommy. He couldn't walk down the aisle so "Auntie Lily," as she called herself, would carry him. Tessa was thrilled that the young woman was going to stay in Tommy's life. Tessa leaned forward and kissed the baby's cheeks.

"I think it's your turn," she said. "I'll see you up there."

Lily started the slow procession of carrying Tommy down the aisle. Once they got to the front and the baby spotted Luke, he dove out of Lily's arms right into his father's waiting hold. The entire congregation laughed. The little one had not diminished in his obsession for Luke. He had fostered Tommy for the past several months. They were waiting on the adoption finalization from a judge.

Luke was still the number one person Tommy wanted holding him, whether he was happy or sad. Tessa couldn't take her eyes off her boys as she walked down the aisle. She loved both of them so much. Luke looked so handsome in his tux, and Tommy was wearing a matching baby version.

Thomas gave Tessa a kiss on the cheek before handing her off to Luke. "I'm so happy we get to keep you," he said.

Tessa beamed at him and joined her soon-to-be husband in front of the pastor. They said their vows to each other and sealed them with their first kiss as a married couple, but before they were declared husband and wife, there was an interruption.

"Wait!"

The pastor cleared his throat. "Um, we passed the objection part."

An older man stepped up next to him, a bunch of paperwork in his hands. "Oh, I'm not here to object. I'm here to make this ceremony more complete."

"This is a surprise from your friend Sierra, but we're ready to finalize your adoption of Tommy here today."

Luke gasped. "Really? We can do that now?"

The judge nodded and turned to Tessa, who had also had agreed to adopt Tommy in the future. "You both can."

"Yes, of course, we would love to," Tessa said.

The judge made both of them raise their right hands and swear to love, care for and protect Tommy and to legally become his parents. They both said "I do" to that promise. The judge produced some paperwork and they signed it. Tessa couldn't believe it was that easy.

The judge made to step down, but Luke stopped him. "Wait, wait, there's one more thing you can do while you're up here."

He turned to the front row. "Zack, can you come up here, buddy?"

Zack looked at them with wide eyes as he approached the stage. Poor guy hadn't found a long-term placement or forever family yet. Tessa had a sneaking suspicion it was because Luke had yet again not approved anyone for him. She had teased him. "You know you can't keep each one of these kids that are special to you. It doesn't work that way. You have to learn to let them go."

But not today, it seemed. She grinned, thinking of the conversation about this they'd had with Sierra a few weeks back. When Zack made it to the front, Luke squatted down until he was eye level with the boy.

"Hey, Zack, do you want to be part of our family? Can we adopt you, too, buddy? Can I be your dad?"

Zack looked like he had just been offered a million bucks. "Really? You want to be my dad?"

Luke reached out and put his hand on the boy's shoulder. "Yeah, I sure do, buddy. I want to flip pancakes with you and play catch with you. And have you be my sidekick while I'm fixing things," Luke said. "And not to mention, Tommy needs a big brother to show him how the world works."

Zack nodded enthusiastically. "I will be the absolute best big brother in the whole world."

Tessa ruffled the boy's hair. "Oh, we know you will, and you're going to be the best son."

At that, the boy turned to Tessa. "You're gonna be my mom."

The awe in his voice melted her heart. She knew exactly how he felt going from being alone in the world to having a family of his own. "Yeah, bud, I want to be your mom."

Tessa turned to the judge. "We filed the paperwork a couple of weeks ago. Do you think maybe we could do this today too?"

The judge locked eyes with Sierra, who nodded before stepping off the stage to her bag that was stashed on the front row. She pulled a bunch of papers out of her bag. "I thought this might be the turn of events, so I just happened to be prepared."

Tessa hugged her friend after she handed the paperwork to the judge.

"Okay, you know how this goes. Raise your right hands… again."

The pair of them vowed to love and care for Zack as their own. Her heart was full knowing he wouldn't have to move to another home again.

The other foster kids in the front row stood on their chairs and shouted with excitement. Tessa wished she could adopt them all, but she knew there were forever families waiting for them someday.

The rest of the congregation was filled with familiar faces who had come to mean so much to her in the past six months as they supported Harmony House and her kids with their all.

The judge and pastor may have just made them an official family, but they already had been one for a while. In her quest to prove that she could run the foster home by herself, she ended up with a husband and two sons by her side instead. From now on, she would learn to expect the unexpected when it came to God's interference with their plans.

"I now pronounce you…a family," the judge said, and the audience went wild.

* * * * *

If you liked this story from Julie Brookman, check out her previous Love Inspired books:

Their Business Betrothal
His Temporary Family

Available now from Love Inspired!

Find more great reads at www.LoveInspired.com.

Dear Reader,

Thank you for joining me for another one of my stories! Luke and Tessa have a special place in my heart because in this book, they go above and beyond for children who need love and support the most.

I adopted three children from the foster care system, and throughout that journey, I encountered so many people who had a heart for taking care of little ones who were enduring some of the worst moments of their lives.

It takes special people to fill that need—and I believe Luke and Tessa fit that bill. However, they do it in very different ways that don't always mesh! I hope you enjoy their story and grow to love them as much as I do.

Happy reading!

Julie Brookman